THE NARCISSIST'S DAUGHTER

A Novel

CRAIG HOLDEN

SIMON & SCHUSTER
NEW YORK   LONDON   TORONTO   SYDNEY

SIMON & SCHUSTER
Rockefeller Center
1230 Avenue of the Americas
New York, NY 10020

SIMON & SCHUSTER and colophon are registered trademarks
of Simon & Schuster, Inc.

For information about special discounts for bulk purchases,
please contact Simon & Schuster Special Sales at
1-800-456-6798 or business@simonandschuster.com

Designed by Jan Pisciotta

Manufactured in the United States of America

10   9   8   7   6   5   4   3   2   1

Library of Congress Cataloging-in-Publication Data

Holden, Craig.
The narcissist's daughter / Craig Holden.
p. cm.
1. Fathers and daughters—Fiction. 2. Children of the rich—Fiction.
3. College students—Fiction. 4. Social classes—Fiction. 5. Rich people—Fiction.
6. Revenge—Fiction. 7. Ohio—Fiction. I. Title
PS3558.O347747N37 2005
813'.54—dc22   2004056646

ISBN 0-7432-1297-5

For Arabella

THE
NARCISSIST'S
DAUGHTER

PART ONE

Do you think she's beautiful? Do you think she talks too much? Don't you like her legs?

—JOHN CHEEVER,
Falconer (1975)

ONE

On Tuesday and Friday mornings in the spring of 1979, end of that era of denim suits and leather sport coats and, of course, disco, I had a class called Ethics. I didn't care much for the vagueness of the humanities but the pre-med degree required a certain number of hours in the liberal arts and old Dr. Masterson, my semiretired adviser, had suggested this one. I didn't see how these obscure discussions would help one day when I had to decide whether to pull the plug on some poor failed body but it wasn't especially difficult to read the texts and fill up the blue books.

The campus was nearly walking distance from the city's estate section, which, as it happened after class one fine warm musk-on-the-air heart-of-spring Friday morning, I drove into. I'd learned a few days earlier that my boss, or rather the boss of my boss, the chief of us all in the hospital laboratory where I worked, had flown to Miami, Florida. Since I happened to know that his brother lived in Coral Gables, I took this to mean it was a family thing, that they'd all be down there, the wife and the daughter as well. I'd been fantasizing for weeks on their ruination, even to the extent of envisioning various bloody scenarios of murder. (I'm ashamed now to admit that but I knew really that what I wanted was to see them in some living hell rather than the painless void of death, and anyway killing in the abstract isn't so hard to consider, death having no stench in daydreams. I have in the intervening years come to know a few things about the stench of death.) The truth was that the particular mechanism of how to bring about this happy end, the destruction of the Ted Kesslers, hadn't exactly occurred to me yet; I had no idea really even in which direction it might lie. They were an unassailable monolith, moneyed and beautiful and installed high in the city's society, but it was by-god pleasing to pass the stultifying hours in Ethics dreaming about fucking those people up.

Their great grand house lay in the oldest part of the estate section on a narrow red-brick lane lined with oak trees and set deeply back in a grove of more oaks and evergreens and a single ancient willow that wept over all of it. It was built of brick and painted white, with a turret and a shale roof and a huge ever-fresh wreath of woven sprigs on the front door, and in the back sat a wide three-bay two-story garage with swinging doors and a smaller turret of its own. It was all something from a dream, a place you could have spent your life, with its weathered wood-slatted furniture and sunlight-dappled pathways and glens, its vines and mossy trees. I first saw it late the previous fall and remember wondering then and each of the many times I saw it again throughout that winter what it must look like when it greened. Well, here it was now before me, blossomed, fleshed out, sprung.

It'd rained through the night and the grass and the new leaves shined (even the tire wounds I'd made to the turf the month before had nearly healed). In addition to the city cruisers, private cops also patrolled these neighborhoods but the curtain of trees was so dense as to render the house barely visible from the road, and who would suspect anything anyway? I was clean and trimmed of hair, obviously just a friend of the family over to check on their profusion of stuff while they were away, to make sure nothing looked awry. I stepped out into the wet earthy scents of that Eden and oh, the colors vibrated, even the wide black driveway glistened like something new.

The fact was that the simple act of putting my feet on that asphalt constituted a violation and, pathetic and inconsequential as it would probably end up being, I meant it as one. I trembled. It felt strangely like when I'd arrived for each of those earlier visits (that thudding of the heart, that thickness in the throat, that anticipatory scrotal tingling). Here finally I stood again breathing where she breathed, in proximity to the things she touched and looked upon every day, to where she slept and bathed and dressed though she, Joyce, the doctor's wife, my one-time co-worker, my confidant, my playmate, was herself gone far away from it just then.

I wondered if they kept a key under a mat or some other obvious place. The truth was I didn't know if I'd dare do anything more than look around a little, but just that, the looking, the bare fact of being there unbidden, was something, and the simple possibility of doing more, of polluting them in some way, of my malice becoming manifest instead of this awful closeted gnawing made my barren inner landscape begin to feel as verdant again as the real world around me. Then as I stood before the big house a new fantasy came on—of me, Syd Redding, going through her things.

The front walkway was a mosaic constructed of heavy pieces of slate (some with a greenish cast, some pink, some gray). I remember wondering what this alone must have cost. I peered up at the glistening slate roof and then, as I walked along the edge of the porch examining the perfect shrubberies, the dog, Dog, barked. Inside the house. I moved back toward the front door, the realization of what his yappy presence meant just crystallizing in my brain when the door cracked open and Jessi Kessler (the daughter, sole progeny of the doctor and the nurse) gazed out at me.

I knew her. I mean, I'd met her. She was seventeen, a senior in high school. I hated her the least of the three of them and only really because she was *of* them. In a vacuum I'd have just found her mildly irritating.

"What are you doing here?" she said.

I could feel the crimson rising like tequila suns in my cheeks. "Um, I had something for your mom."

"What?"

"A book."

She waited, watching me.

I said, "We were talking, you know, at work, at the hospital, about stuff, and I said I had this book, and she said she wanted to read it. But I haven't seen her around." (My god, I could lie in those years, just open my mouth and let it run out with no forethought, no planning or conniving at all.)

"She doesn't work there anymore."

"Oh?" I said. "Well, anyway, I happened to be over here and I thought I'd just drop it off."

"She's not here. She's with my dad in Florida."

"Well, it's not a big deal."

"Where is it?"

"The book? Um, in my car."

"You can leave it if you want."

I went back and opened the door and made a pretense of looking in but I knew there was nothing—even then I liked my spaces clean. I closed the door and glanced at her and opened the trunk, which held, aside from a tool kit and a box of emergency supplies and a spare tire, only my notebook and the texts from the class I'd just had. I picked up the smallest one, a paperback of the *Nichomachean Ethics,* and carried it to her.

"My mother wants to read Aristotle?"

"Well, I don't know. We were just talking about it."

"*Aristotle?*"

"Ethics. You know. The hospital?"

She looked at me blankly, she in her too-big corduroys and black T-shirt and a different pair of glasses than when I'd seen her before, heavy ones, these, with ugly black oval frames that somehow flattered her. She had a finely boned face, pretty despite the extra poundage she carried. (It was just the last remnants of the plumpness of her youth, that weight, and would burn off with her final sprint into adulthood, leaving her every bit as unjustly arresting, as beautiful even, as her mother.)

"Fix any cars lately?" she said. It was a kind of joke between us. We met the previous November when I spotted her and her mother broken down along Cherry Street just outside St. V's, our mutual employer (Joyce and I worked the night shift together then, I in her husband's lab as I've said and she as an ICU nurse, part time), and stopped to help.

"Not really," I said. "Just keeping mine going." We paused to glance at the old thing, a rusted military-green Datsun 610, embarrassingly incongruous in that driveway in that neighborhood—even the hired help around there, the maids and nannies and gardeners, had nicer rides than mine.

"I just got a new Cutlass Supreme," she said.

"Really?"

"Early graduation present."

"Wow."

"Yeah. It's kind of sick, isn't it? You want to see it?" She tossed the book into the house, stepped into a pair of Sorels, and walked out past me. Dog came after her and stopped to sniff my ankles.

"You must smell nice," she said over her shoulder. "He usually growls at strangers."

We followed her across the driveway and through the gate and out back to the garage. She swung open one of the high doors and there it gleamed in all its American newness, a pearly bluish gray with a navy landau roof and the stickers still pasted in the rear window. The license plate said Path 3. I couldn't imagine owning something like this then, at twenty-three, let alone at seventeen.

"What's weird," she said, "is how much I like it, and how much I hate liking it, you know? I really didn't want to like it but it's like a new pet or something, or a different life. Here." She opened the driver's door and waved me around.

"That's a new car," she said, sniffing deeply. I'd never smelled one before that I could remember, if you can believe it. It was upholstered in gray chamois-soft leather but she let Dog jump onto her lap and from there into the backseat, where he began rooting around.

"It's beautiful," I said. It was, truly. I just couldn't quite accept it yet that I was sitting there chatting with the little pudge when I'd come over to maybe do something awful or at least distasteful, a little B and E or just some childish vandalism.

"It's what I get for having to put up with him." Her father, she meant, of course—I looked at her, unsure whether she was being funny or not. "He's a narcissist, so he compensates like this, you know. If you can't give love, give new cars. It must suck working for him."

"I don't really see him much anymore. I work nights."

"That's lucky."

"I mean, I did work days, but I moved as soon as they let me."

"Because of him?"

I shrugged. "Not just him."

"Yeah," she said. She pushed the cigarette lighter in, and when it popped back out she said, "You know I got in at Case."

"Hey. Congratulations."

"I still haven't committed."

"When's the deadline?"

"In like a week."

"Are you going?"

"I don't know. I suppose. He went there, so, you know, Daughter has to." They weren't much for given names, that family. I don't know if I ever heard any of them refer to each other by anything other than pronouns or the most general nouns, He or She or Wife or Husband or Dog (which was truly the little shit's actual registered name—Joyce showed me the official papers one time; I asked and she told me how much he'd cost, which was substantially more than my car, and him looking exactly like nothing so much as a slightly used mop with feet).

"It's a pretty great school," I said. I'd gotten in, too, once. I had, it turned out (to everyone's surprise) a bit of an aptitude for numbers and the natural sciences. I don't know where it came from. I mean, I'd always done well enough in those subjects but no one ever accused me of being a genius. Then I popped a 780 on the math section of the SATs and all the world, a world that had never seemed to know I was there, began suddenly to regard me. Teachers stopped me in the hallway to chat. Girls who'd never spoken to me started to fawn. And colleges, lots of them, began sending me packets. But things turned another way and I ended up staying here, working crap jobs and picking off a couple classes a semester at the local university, the U of T.

This went on until Masterson (who had a scout's eye for talent and found me in my first month on campus and recruited me as med school material) called the previous summer to say that the lab at St. V's, the huge medical center in the north downtown ghetto, was looking to train a group of pre-med students in phlebotomy, the ancient art of bloodletting, and to employ them weekdays six to nine A.M. to help with the deluge of routine morning draws. It paid six bucks an hour at a time when the minimum wage was something like $2.50, so just like that I became a health care professional with my own frighteningly white lab coat and, after I went to nights, made enough to swing school full time.

"I guess," Jessi said. "It doesn't seem too exciting. He wants me to go pre-med but I see so many assholes like him, I just don't want to be around that. I mean—" She glanced at me. "You're pre-med, aren't you?"

"Yeah."

"I didn't mean—"

"No, I understand. I know what you mean."

"Anyway, I don't know if that's my thing or not. And I feel like bumming around Europe or something first." She popped a cassette out of the deck and looked at it, then put it back. She said, "Where have you applied?"

"I haven't, yet. I'm only a junior."

"How old are you?"

"Old."

She nodded. "You want some coffee or something?"

"I should get going. I didn't mean to bug you."

"It's all right. I'm just hanging out. I'm having a party tonight I was sort of getting ready for."

"Getting ready?"

"Actually, I just didn't feel like facing school today. My friends mostly aren't from there. I don't really even like any of those people, you know?" She looked over and said, "Hey, you should come tonight. It's not going to be some stupid high school blowout with a bunch of drunken jocks. We cook and stuff, listen to good music, drink some good wine. It'll be cool."

Could this be it, then, oh, irony of ironies—my entrée? In exchange for suffering her insipid friends for a few hours, I'd be one giant leap closer to slipping off to do whatever it was I decided to do, plant a bomb or sprinkle itching powder in their beds or shave Dog or some other as yet unimagined degradation.

"Seriously?"

"Yeah," she said. "It'd be a trip if you showed up."

When I got home I saw my neighbor Donny Tooman lying in the street with his feet and lower legs sticking out from beneath a car. Well, it was his car (a '69 Road Runner 426 hemi to which he'd added so far an Edelbrock manifold and a Ram Air cam, and painted a metallic fire-hydrant yellow), and that was where he worked on it, his mother's single-car garage being reserved for the new Buick she bought every third June, so he always just lay there in the stones with the thing up on jack stands to do his business. It was perhaps the headiness that had come of my unexpected triumph at the doctor's house (talk about your foot in the door) but I felt suddenly resolved to rectify not only my personal grievances but all the fucking aggravations and wrongs and injustices I knew of. It felt as if I'd been sitting watching for too long and now something needed to be done, or rather had always needed to be done but was left for me to do because clearly no one else was going to lift a finger.

I walked over to the Road Runner and stomped on Donny's booted ankle.

"Hey!" he shouted. He slid out and looked up at me. "S'up your ass?"

"Lay off her."

"What you talking about?"

"You know what I'm talking about, Donny. I don't know what you've done or how long it's been going on or whatever you think you have a right to but I'll tell you this—it ends right now, right here. Or I will seriously *seriously* fuck you up."

He stared up at me. Blankly, you might say. He was as vacuous a human being as I had ever met.

"Syd—" he started.

"No," I said, "I don't want to talk about it. I don't want to hear any denials or excuses or justifications. I'm telling you, I find out you so much as touched her after this, I'll tie you down and take Brigman's ax and chop your hand off at the wrist."

"Jesus Christ—"

"—will not help you in this, Donny."

I crossed back over to our place, one in a line of tall and narrow clapboard deals on a tarred and graveled dead end street in the old south end. It had been not so long before that a prosperous enough looking place, both the house and the neighborhood, I mean, but it had all changed somehow along with our circumstances. When I was seventeen—recipient of dozens of come-hither co-eds-lounging-on-the-grassy-green brochures from colleges around the country; on the very verge of beginning to realize my one true ambition, my goal-since-childhood, which was not actually then to be a doctor but just to be somebody—my stepfather, Brigman Reed (my younger sister Chloe's actual father), was in a bad car wreck. It was largely a result of his own carelessness, for which he would spend six months in the can after his release from the hospital, and he would never really quite recover from it, but it affected me directly because I put off college for a year to stick around and help out at home. By the time Brigman got out, our mother, Sandy, had been diagnosed with metastasized lung cancer, of which she died not long after I turned nineteen. Things had kind of been falling apart ever since. Now, in Sandy's absence (as if she had somehow personally held all of it together) each of the nearly identical houses seemed to lean to one side or the other, and you noticed peeling paint and curling shingles and rotting-leaf-carpeted lawns where there had once been only neatness and care. As for my ambitions—which had by then, with Masterson's encouragement and as a reaction I think now to the serial crises of Brigman's accident and my mother's illness, lit on medicine—they stayed hot as ever in the heart of my heart. But time, of course, hurried on, so it was only now, after the break of getting the lab job, after I had finally been able to go back to school full time, that I felt on the verge again of my life.

As I came up the front concrete steps I did the dance—knees urgently flexed, hand grasping for the nonexistent railing, swearing under the breath (they'd cracked down the middle so they shifted when you stepped on them and for an instant made you think you were falling)—and came into our shit-stuffed living room. A television alcove jutted out beside the porch, so there should have been plenty of space for furniture, but after Sandy died Brigman (which is all I'd ever called him from the time he and my mom started dating when I was eight) began filling it with stuff he refused for whatever reason to throw out (cardboard boxes of her clothing, stacks of newspapers and magazines, cases of empty beer bottles, the broken remains of Chloe's childhood toys) so now the television sat in the square middle of the room, on boxes, and the two easy chairs were shoved back against the wall and you had to make your way through it all on pathways that had been hewn out between the piles.

Chloe stood inside the door, arms folded over the breast-shelf of her chest, glaring at me. She'd obviously seen or anyway heard my little tirade of threats to her special friend, our forever neighbor-across-the-street, he who was twenty-four to her sixteen.

She said, "You prick."

"Great," I said. "Nice to see you, too. How's your day been, Chlo?"

She was born, my baby sister, with a facial disfigurement called a nevus flammeus, what you might hear called a port-wine stain, just a birthmark really but in her case a huge one—it covered half her face (the right half, as it happened) from the midline of her mouth and chin up across her cheek to just above her eye and nearly over to her ear—that darkened as she grew from infancy until by the time she was toddling it was the color I would call magenta, that is, the shade of a just ripening plum when its dark redness has begun to be shot through with a deeper richer violet. It was the crisis of her life, of course, that mask, a horrid torment for a girl who had always been pretty otherwise.

Now, on top of it, she was newly built in a way that made your heart hurt—well, it made my heart hurt but pretty much every other man's neck twist. Chloe had a bosom, you might say, the sort that even other women appraised. It only compounded the view she had of herself as freakish, as a creature the world had license to regard shamelessly and openly.

She said, "Why can't you just mind your own business?"

What does a girl from a collapsed and hopeless place do when she has a bicolored face and a body that stops traffic? Where does she turn when she has no mother and the shadow of a father and a brother who's utterly preoccupied with his own perceived miseries and injustices, and she wants so terribly just to have friends, to be let in? How does she accomplish that? It's not a hard question to answer. Chloe had not wanted, since the time she was in junior high, for boyfriends, at least.

"Night," I said, and headed up the stairs. I was exhausted. I'd worked the night before, gone straight to class, run a reconnaisance mission that turned into a face-to-face with the enemy and led, quite unexpectedly, to a penetration of their peripheral defenses, so that now apparently I had ahead of me another long night, though of a wholly different sort.

I barely even heard it when Chloe shouted after me, "Why do you have to go around making everyone miserable?"

TWO

The lab, which occupied two entire wings of the basement of the main hospital building, was actually a private corporation owned by four pathologists, three of whom we rarely saw and who looked and acted as you might guess (as I guessed) people who work with the dead and disembodied would—they were gnomish men who locked themselves into their laboratory offices and spent the days staring at tissue samples and blood cells and writing reports about what they saw, or over in the small autopsy room in a distant part of the basement. The fourth, though, was Dr. Kessler, who ran it all, and this job of administrator, politician, enforcer, facilitator, even cheerleader seemed to suit him in ways I imagined the more typical and pedestrian chores of a clinical pathologist did not (though he was widely acknowledged to be brilliant at such things). He also owned a piece of an outside lab that served nursing homes and clinics and offices, lectured at the medical school and around the region, researched and wrote and published, and sat on several hospital boards.

Though he had Ph.D.s under him to manage the departments, and technologists under them to run all the sections, and though the phlebotomists were in general the undegreed serfs and riffraff of the lab, Ted seemed from the beginning to take a strangely ar-

dent interest in those of us who came in from the university. After
we'd finished our training, he made a point every week that fall on
a Thursday or Friday of taking a couple of us upstairs to breakfast.
Most of the other students were a bare step beyond adolescence
and spoiled on top of that (middle-white-collar-class kids looking
to get into the upper middle or rich kids looking to stay that way)
and I ignored them to the extent I could. I was aware, though, of
the hissing speculation among the as yet unfed about what it must
mean if you got asked to one of these breakfasts—that it was a kind
of interview that could lead to Kessler writing a letter of recom-
mendation (which was given to be virtually tantamount to an ad-
mission somewhere). The thought of such a letter made my arm
hairs stand up. These spoiled young were unabashed about clawing
like cats for advantage: refusing to divulge anything they'd learned
about Kessler; spreading trash behind each other's backs; stealing
draw-lists to get a more challenging set in order to show off or an
easier one to finish quickly and be available for an invitation. I
didn't play these games, though not because I had any less ambition
or desire. On the contrary it made me almost blind to think they
might get over on me. Still, with the additional curing I had on
them I thought I understood something about the value of subtlety,
of just not appearing to be an asshole. So I waited.

And one morning a month or so later—it was the fall now of
1978—I got down from the floors early along with a couple of the
other students and two of the regular day-shift full-timers. I was
at the supply rack replenishing my tray with all the variously stop-
pered test tubes—brick red, sky blue, turtle green, gray, lavender,
and even the rarely used navy (for lead levels)—when the room
behind me went suddenly quiet. "Morning, girls," Dr. Kessler
said. I turned around as his glance swept across the others to me
and he winked.

"Let's grab some grub," he barked, not a question or an offer,
but a command. The black lady regulars who knew the order
didn't include them clicked and tssked and mmmed as we students
followed him into the hallway.

He was a compact man, slender, not tall, darkly complected, and always perfectly groomed. Though he wore a trimmed mustache in a nod perhaps to the relaxed fashions of the time, he still had his hair cut crew as he had since the days of his military service in Korea. He wore expensive suits and vests and ties under his lab coat; his teeth were large and white and his skin unnaturally clean and scrubbed. He was beyond forty-five then but had done well at keeping himself from looking it. The other salient thing about him was that his right hand was a hook, a split hook, actually, operated by cables attached somehow farther up his arm, which he used as dexterously as if it had grown there—I'd seen him manipulate test tubes with it and once watched him accept a glass slide from someone and hold it by its edges up to the light.

After taking our scrambled eggs and toast we followed him across the open cafeteria to a plain blond wooden door that said, in small important letters, Physicians' Dining Room. The doctors in their suits or lab coats and scrubs glanced up at us, then away again and I, noticing some frowns, felt like the trespasser I was (even escorted we were no way allowed in there) but I had the sense that Ted would have loved for one of them to challenge him and for us to witness that exchange. Of course he knew no one would, though I didn't know it at the time.

We took a corner table and after the predictable how-are-classes and when-do-you-graduate b.s. it segued into Ted going on about his own college and military experiences and what hospitals were like in those old-seeming days of the Eisenhower 50s, the two girls nodding and beaming and barely touching their food they were so busy making sure he could see that they were sucking it up. I was starved; I ate and looked around the room (which was nicely carpeted and wallpapered and lamp-lighted like a living room) at the Rolex watches and silk ties and Florsheim shoes. One older doc sucked prissily on a pipe with an ornate meerschaum bowl carved into the shape of a man's head; another wore a sport coat of some kind of coarse woven material that was meant to be hip and was undoubtedly absurdly expensive but looked absurd on his paunchy shortish middle-aged carcass. I was tuned in to all of it and, hungry as I was for the food, I was hungrier still for that stuff—no, not the stuff itself really, but the ability to have it, to be able to simply point and say, "That."

Perhaps because I was so full of it, such an expert on Want, or because I had been working around the privileged enough by then to have come to know the look of their longing, it came to me clearly that Dr. Kessler, who from my vantage could have anything he chose, who was probably among the richest dozen doctors in the entire city, was as consumed by it as I was, that we were kindred spirits in desire. For one thing he was too earnest— the girls and I were only undergraduates, we had no standing in anything, we were too far down the ladder to even be considered as protégés. And he was no mere pathologist, being himself practically an institution. You might assume as I did initially that it was just generosity, his way of giving something back, but the more I watched him the more I knew I was right. He wanted something from us.

When we'd ridden back downstairs and the girls walked off ahead of us, I felt a tug on my right bicep and looked down to see that the point of Ted's hook had snagged me. He said, "You didn't say much up there, Syd."

I shrugged. "Thanks for breakfast."

"That, you already said. Don't be too grateful for things. So how's it all going? Did I hear you're working another job besides this one?"

"I wait tables at the Armour Country Club."

"Ah," he said and regarded me as if something had slipped into place. "What about your classes? Masterson tells me you started Organic this semester as well."

I nodded.

"Can you handle everything?"

"It's a lot of work."

"Well, I know how that goes."

"Are you a member?" At the club, I meant. I'd never seen him there.

"I write them a check every year, though I don't know why. Who's got time to golf?"

"I know," I said. "I have the same problem."

He smiled, then said, "You from around here?"

"Yeah."

"What do your folks do?"

"My step-dad used to be a tool-and-die maker at Hydramatic and my mom was the first woman line supervisor they ever had."

"Is that right? My old man was a pipe fitter up at the Rouge." Ford. I couldn't have guessed that, of course, but it thrilled me, this sort of connection between us, however faint. The sons of autoworkers. "We lost him just last year."

"Yeah. My mom's gone."

He'd had to work for it, too—that's what it was, I figured. He'd had to fight his way up and it mattered, even now, even from the pinnacle where he lived, to have that understood.

Then, apropos of nothing, he said, "You ever think about nights?"

"To work?" The thought of hauling into class on no sleep didn't sound like much of a good idea.

"There's going to be an opening soon. Your probation'll be up here in another few weeks. Consider it. Better hourly than you're making now, and more hours. Some benefits. Your days free. You could quit the club."

I nodded.

"Okay," he said, as if he'd taken my nod as an assent.

I said, "No. I mean . . . I'll think about it."

His eyes held hard on mine, not blinking. They were pale, almost amber. He stepped in closer. "Can you get through Organic?" he said. "I don't mean As. Just survive it."

"I'll get an A."

"Will you?"

"Yes."

"Then why do you always look so worried to me?"

I could smell his Hi Karate. He looked up and down the hallway as if he were going to tell me some secret that mustn't be overheard and said, "It wasn't random, you know, your getting hired here. We didn't just pull names out of a hat. You were recommended and vetted. It's not only about grades. I mean, you've got a long way to go, some big hurdles. But you're in the system now." He lifted his eyebrows as if to say, Dig?

I nodded.

"It's really a question," he said, "from here on out, of just not fucking up." He smiled. "Listen, you have anything on your mind, want a word, drop by my office."

"Sure. Thanks."

He touched the front of my lab coat with his hook, then said, "Gotta go," and hurried away down the hallway.

Past the blur of that initial month I began to discern the hierarchy of the lab, that is, which technologists would remain on the bench for their careers and which would become management—it had everything to do with Dr. Kessler. He was the sun, and the techs the astral bodies that revolved around him (some of them among the most egregious ass-kissers I'd ever met).

Barb Lancioni, who was only maybe two years older than me, was the day-shift phlebotomy supervisor. She'd been a bench chemist for a few years out of college before the bump up to management and still had a lot to prove. Often at the end of my short shift when things had settled from the morning rush into the steadier pace of the rest of the day, I'd pass Ted's office and see Barb in there laughing wildly at something he'd said, or leaning in to enlighten him about some sin another tech had committed. Barb was one of the detachment of snitches (the chief one, I gathered) whose fierce loyalty Ted had inspired. He had that ability to rouse people to service, stir them to great heights of commitment. He was a motivator. His snitch brigade was scattered throughout the various departments and their extra unspoken duty was to keep him apprised of everything that was going on. You could tell when they had something to feed him—they got all nervous. With

Barb it was always a high flush in her gauntish cheeks as if her very temperature had risen in anticipation of basking in his glow.

One morning I passed his opened door as he sat at his desk, reading, and glanced in at him at the precise moment he happened to look up.

"Syd," he said.

I paused, or froze, and nodded and said, "Dr. Kessler."

"Come on in. Sit."

The hallway was empty and I was glad of that. I wanted very much not to seem like one of them, the snitches, and had the strong urge to shut the door behind me, though I resisted it.

"So how's Organic?"

"B on the first exam."

"That'll work."

I shook my head and he smiled. Behind him was a built-in alcove with a work shelf that held a heavy binocular microscope. "You know there're some pretty smart people down here who could help you out, if you want."

"Tutoring?"

"You don't have to call it that. Just someone to run compounds with you. Someone who's smart about it. I could ask around."

His asking, of course, would render it so. I nodded vaguely in acknowledgment of the possibility, and again he seized on that as my agreement, and said, "All right, then. I'll find someone." He looked at me for a moment, then leaned across his desk and said, "Are you seeing anyone?"

"What?"

"A girlfriend."

"Oh. No," I said, "not at the moment."

"Have you thought more about third shift? We really need someone."

I started to nod, then caught myself and said, "Not really."

"It's a good job for someone in your position. I mean, in school and all, working your way through."

I watched him.

"How's the club?"

"Same."

"I imagine. What do you do, wait tables?"

"Bus, wash dishes."

"You like that kind of work?"

"No."

He shook his head and practically glared at me for not leaping at this fine offer. And it was fine. I knew that. I'd be in more deeply with him than these other putz students, a real working member of the lab, not to mention making more money. But something in his very earnestness, his insistence on bringing it up and shoving it at me again, as if he'd already decided what was best for me and now had only the minor inconvenience of convincing me to move on it, put me off. In a way it frightened me.

Then he leaned back, put his arms over his head, and gripped the hook with his good hand. "I didn't date much in college, either. No time. Didn't meet my wife until I was almost through med school—Case Western, did I say that?—and even that was sooner than I'd planned on getting involved, sooner than I wanted, but, well, you'd have to know her. You'd understand. Anyway, you're young. Plenty of time."

"Not that young."

"Oh, yes, I forget that you're the old man of the group. I went through late, too, you know. Korea." He let the hook go and held it out in front of him, as if it offered some kind of explanation.

"I've just been working."

"That's better than getting your ass shot at."

And I heard it there again, or maybe it was the way he looked at me—but I caught that hint of a desire for something.

"Does it bother you," I asked, "talking about it?"

"This? No. Old news. But it's an ugly story."

"Yeah?"

Now I was the one to lean forward, feigning fascination. He had work to do and I had class but he couldn't help himself as I had known he would not be able to. He talked for a long time and it occurred to me that I was doing what I knew how to do, and what was necessary, and also how transparent things became in the world when you had been in it long enough. He should've seen my ruse but maybe he'd been away from the street too long and his edges were dulled now, so he didn't recognize a manipulation, or maybe as I'd thought before he just didn't care.

It wasn't that ugly, as it turned out, but I ate it up.

One night soon after that I was struck with a violent stomach flu. I eventually managed to call the night shift clerk to say I wouldn't be in that morning, stopped heaving sometime around four, and fell into a coma-like sleep. I didn't wake until nearly noon. The following morning when I came down from my rounds, Barb hooked a finger at me from the door of Ted's office. He sat impassively behind his desk, hand over hook upon it while she informed me that I was being written up for not calling in. A write-up was a serious reprimand; two in a six-month period could lead to dismissal.

"But I did call in," I said.

She wagged a bitchy finger and said that, no, in fact, I had not. It was my responsibility to inform her *directly,* not to rely on someone from the night shift to do it for me. She came in early, at five o'clock, for precisely that reason.

I looked at Dr. Kessler (not quite believing this) and when he just nodded, a wave of the dizziness of disbelief, of the spank of surreality, struck me. The room felt suddenly small and hot and too close to breathe in.

"It's not fair," I said. "I called."

"This is a complex place, Syd," Kessler said. "Only by rules and protocols is it able to function at all."

What assholes! And him a flake on top of it, so driven by the itch of the moment, which just then apparently was to play god for the benefit of his little hanger-on. His side-squeeze. His spare piece of ass (oh, I'd heard that rumor more than once and found it plenty easy to believe). I felt set up and betrayed, and had the urge to tell them both to fuck off.

But I'd just had a birthday that month and was looking at what I saw as my last shot at what I wanted most. Even through the haze of my rage I managed not to lose sight of that. I hastened out into the hallway to get away from them, and practically ran into a night-shift tech named Ray Vollmer who seemed to know just from looking at me what was up.

"You off?" he said.

"Not till nine."

"You know Ziggy's up on Madison?"

"I guess so. Yeah."

"Meet me."

It was a small dirty place and I drank quickly. Ray laughed while I fumed, then told me about the opening for a phlebotomy tech on thirds.

"Jesus," I said, "Kessler's been pushing it at me."

"Well, take it," Ray said. "Get away from him and the rest of those pricks. Nights are great, man. You'd love it."

And for a moment, a brief sodden flash, I saw it all—Barb knocks me down and Ray's there to pick me up and point me where Ted has already decided I'm going to go. I've been motivated.

And for a minute I believed it, and seethed. But only for a minute. I mean, really. Why would Ted Kessler spend a single one of his golden moments thinking about me, let alone conspiring?

The next morning Ray introduced me to Phyllis Myers, the night supervisor. I had a week left in my probationary period, so she couldn't offer me the job until then, but she made it clear it was mine if I wanted. I had time to think, though there wasn't much to think about. It would be four shifts, thirty-two hours a week, with a pay increase and a shift differential to boot. I'd take home more than I was now from both jobs combined, and be eligible for the hospital's tuition reimbursement plan on top of that. And still I thought about refusing it. But it would have been so purely out of some kind of misguided spite that even I knew how foolish it would be. I took it.

Dr. Kessler stopped me one morning shortly after I'd made the decision and said, "This'll be good for you. And for us. I appreciate it."

I nodded.

"I'm glad it's shaping up for you. Oh, and listen, I found someone to help with the Organic. You know Kathy Rudner in the Blood Bank? If you can stay after a morning or two a week—"

"Sure. Of course."

"Good." He smiled and turned away, then stopped and turned back. "You know," he said, "my wife works the night shift."

"Here?"

"Yes, she's a nurse." Then he said, "She's something, you know."

"Yeah?"

"You'll have to keep an eye on her for me. Will you do that?"

I had no idea what to say or in what spirit he would make such a comment to someone so far beneath him. He winked at me again before walking off.

THREE

A short woman with red eyes and pendulous hair that swung nearly to her knees opened the front door as I approached—had she been watching for me?—and said, "Hey, man." She led me through the foyer and into the darkened parlor where the smell of burned reefer hung on the air. A woman sang in French from the huge speakers there in a voice so tragic and smoky it seemed like a parody of something except that it was perfect, and though I understood only a little of that language then, I got it.

"How's it goin?" someone said. A few of the people sitting around the room in the chairs and on the couches and the floor looked to be Jessi's age but most were in their twenties, a couple of the men with ponytails. I stood for a minute watching them pass a pipe but thought getting stoned would be a bad idea in that house, to let any sort of unnecessary new paranoia creep in, there being enough generated already by my thinking in the ways I was thinking then, so before it got to me I wandered back into the hallway.

The dining room table held a tray with chunks of cheese and Triscuits and bowls of chips and pretzels and Fritos and an opened container of French onion dip. In the lighted kitchen Jessi peered into the oven. A woman around my age stood beside her holding a glass of white wine while a balding bearded man cut vegetables over the sink. The music played here, too, through smaller speakers set into the walls.

Jessi looked up and said, a little loudly, "*Hey,* there. This is Edith Piaf. I love her."

"Oh," I said and nodded at the other woman, who started to laugh. She said, "I'm Nancy, actually. That's Joel. Edith's the one singing. And Jessi's drunk."

Jessi said, "I am not, you bitch."

"Oh, right," Nancy said, "I forgot."

"Syd's pre-med and he's a tech in my father's lab, so I figured I at least owe him a few beers, in sympathy."

"Really?" Nancy said.

"Well," I said, "just a phlebotomist."

"What's the difference?" Joel asked.

"Really," said Nancy. She took a tray of some melted yellow things from the oven and said, "Dr. Syd, can you carry?" I took it into the dining room and Nancy brought another tray behind me and Jessi and Joel ones behind her, and as if some order had been given, everyone crowded in from the parlor and loaded up plates and then wandered back to find their seats again. Later I volunteered to help clean up the kitchen—I wasn't stoned or drinking very much and was glad of something to do while I waited for my opening. When we were finishing up (Nancy washing, Joel and me drying, Jessi putting away), Joel wiped his hands on a towel and pulled from his front pocket a small brown bottle and sprinkled a mound of white powder on the surface of a glass cutting board. Cocaine was still somewhat exotic at that time, in that place, anyway, and I had never seen it before. He chopped it and cut it into lines with one of Joyce's wooden-block-housed set of German bone-handled steak knives. I watched the others, then sniffed up a line myself, and now instead of paranoid I felt wired. My hands and neck were sweaty, and I wanted to go then and begin tearing the place apart. But I made myself follow the three of them into the parlor and sit.

The dope-smoke cloud had grown thicker; Jessi's eyes glowed like fog lights in it and I couldn't help watching them, her looking as lit up as I felt, and so when yet another lid went around and she hit off it and handed it to me wet from her mouth I took it, of course, and had to hit it too, though shallowly, gently, in order not to get too high but to seem a part of the scene, to camouflage my true status of interloper-cum-coked-up-vandal—but the thing is it was really potent stuff (Maui, someone said) and I didn't smoke much in general and so was sensitive to it, and soon it crept up my neck and over the top of my head and took me in its grip. And for a bleak moment I regretted everything, regretted ever coming here, first for the carnal reasons I'd come before and why I'd come now into a gathering of depressing dopers who were clearly here only because it was a place they could go. I regretted everything I had done practically in my whole life.

Then somewhat abruptly and unexpectedly the chemicals struck a balance and I felt myself relax into it yet remain sharp in my senses, sharp as an absurdly expensive bone-handled coke-cutting steak knife in the modernized kitchen of an old mansion, but calm, too, and ready. Before the balance shifted or faded, I thought, it was time. The beer tasted good to me (these were St. Pauli Girls—you never forget your first girl) and I went out to the kitchen for another one. Then, instead of going back to the parlor, I stopped in the hallway and peered up the wide staircase.

Never had I been so conscious of the creaking of those stairs. But once up, I was alone in the quiet. To get to the master bed-room you passed first through a sitting room, which now held only a couch and a desk. It got darker the farther in I went until, by the time I got to Joyce's dresser, I could hardly see my hand be-fore my face.

I placed my fingertips on the surface and breathed in the faint trace of her perfume, lowered my face to try to see what was there— a tray with bottles on it, I remembered, and a jewelry box. I opened the top right drawer and felt inside—it was all just hard surfaces and edges (small boxes, papers). The next one down held nylons. In the upper left I found her brassieres, and held one up, rubbed my thumbs inside the cups, then put it back. When I felt inside the next drawer down, my breath caught—panties. I plunged my hand into the silky pool and grasped a pair and pulled it out, and knew then what I wanted to do. It didn't solve the problem of my revenge, of what to do to strike some fear or angst or anger into them (I still had no idea) but it felt like just the thing at that moment.

I backed up to the bed and unzipped my jeans. The mere act of baring myself again in that room in that house of course stiffened me right up. I pushed my jeans to my ankles and lay back and began to work the silk vigorously and unceremoniously up and down and was just getting close to the edge, that sudden upramp toward release, when the floorboards creaked and someone at the doorway said, "Hello?"

As calmly as I could manage, I said, "Don't turn on the light."

"All right." It was Jessi.

I found an afghan folded at the foot of the bed and pulled it over myself. I said, "Sorry. I was just being nosy."

"In the dark?"

"Well, then I just felt like lying here. I was tired."

"It's fine," she said. "I don't care."

I thought she'd leave then but she came in and around the bed and sat on the other side.

"I haven't been in here in like a year."

"Why not?"

"They're weird." She huffed and lay back. "I just think they're into weird shit."

"What does that have to do with coming in here?"

"I can *hear* them, you know. In here. And they're in here a lot. And I don't want to, like, accidentally *see* anything."

"You mean them having sex?"

"I can't believe we're talking about this."

I lay back, too, close enough that I could hear her breathing.

"It's other things, too," she said.

"Such as?"

"I don't know. I don't want to talk about it."

"They watch porno or something?"

"Oh, my *god*. How did you know that? Is that like something everyone does?"

"Well, not everyone can afford a video deck or they probably would."

"I mean you can *hear* it, you know? If you listen?"

"So you listen?"

"Well, I mean—no. No! Not like that. God, Syd."

"I'm sorry," I said. We lay for a while then without speaking, me naked under her parents' afghan and her breathing loudly enough that I took it to mean she was pissed off, though not enough apparently to make her leave. Finally she rolled toward me and said, "Do you like Leo Kottke?"

"What?"

"The guitarist?"

"He's all right." I'd never heard of him.

"What do you listen to?"

"Mostly I tape my lectures and listen to those."

"God."

"I know."

"Do you like jazz?"

"Uh, sure."

"Who?"

"I don't really know the names."

"I bet you're into rock."

"Pretty much." Pretty much entirely. I was firmly, that is to say exclusively, of the arena-band head-banger school of that era, Boston, Aerosmith, Sabbath, Thin Lizzy, Queen, Nazareth, Zep, Rush, Mahogany Rush, Uriah Heep, ELO, Nugent, Cheap Trick, Seger, Mott the Hoople, T-Rex, AC/DC, Black Oak Arkansas—I could go on; I'd seen nearly all of them.

"Like?"

"You heard of Van Halen?"

"No."

"They're pretty new."

"Are you into punk? I love the Clash. I *love* the Ramones."

"Some," I said, meaning not at all. I didn't like what little I'd heard of that stuff. My musical taste was really pretty breathtakingly narrow.

The floorboards groaned again and I sat up.

"Who is it?" Jessi said.

"Nancy."

"Don't turn on the light."

"Awww," she said, "I'm telling."

"Shut up," said Jessi.

"Who's with you?"

"Me," I said.

"I knew it," said Nancy. "Don't you two get in any trouble."

"Nancy, god," Jessi said, "we're just talking."

"Sure."

"We *are*."

"Your parents would be so shocked."

"God!" Jessi said.

"All right, all right. Listen, some people are getting ready to take off."

"I'll be down in a minute."

"Have fun," Nancy said. "Bye."

Jessi said, "Anyway—" but I was quiet, distracted by what was then the merest glinting of a reflection cast by what Nancy said— your parents would be so shocked. Imagine, I remember thinking, if she knew the depth of the truth of that statement. The idea didn't come to me then. Not yet. But I would later mark that as the central moment in all that had happened and was about to, as the moment of my becoming.

"I should go down, I guess."

"I'll wait a minute," I said, "so we don't come together. Down, I mean. Stairs."

"Oh, I don't think it matters. But that's fine." She stood up. "You can crash here if you want."

"That's all right."

"Whatever."

When she'd gone, I dressed and was going to put the panties back, then thought better of it and stuffed them in my pocket.

Jessi walked me to my car. The night was warm and as our bare arms brushed, Nancy's comment floated back and I saw it then— my answer, whole, fully formed, delivered unto me like some god-damn apocalypse of insight and cunning and circumstance all come together as if by voodoo. It was perfect; it was exactly poet-ically what they deserved; it would ring their bell more soundingly than almost anything else I could do, than anything I'd thought of short of some pyrrhic act of hyperviolence that would ruin me along with them. It was the sort of dawning that was almost enough to make you believe in something. It even happened (as if the whole thing had been orchestrated, ordained) that I'd driven Brigman's new-old 'Cuda which, when Jessi saw it, inspired her to grab my arm and shriek, "Oh, my god! Is that yours?"

"Sort of."

"It is *amazing*."

"You're into muscle?" (Who knew?)

"I went out with this guy who had a Nova SS so I got to know a lot about it. He even raced some. My parents hated him."

I said, "This one's only got a 340 in it, but it'll be nice when it's ready."

"It looks great now."

"I could take you for a ride sometime."

"For real?"

I waited. I said, "And maybe we could grab a bite or something then."

She laughed, then got quiet. She looked up at me. She said, "Really?"

"Really."

"All right. Yeah. That'd be great."

"Call you?"

"You don't have the number."

"I think I can find it."

"Not my private line."

Ah. I found a pen and she held my hand and wrote on my palm, and then, bracing herself against my arms, reached up and brushed her lips across my cheek. She had that ability to be immediately familiar, the gift of affable touch. But of course she would have, I thought. It was, after all, a part of her endowment.

FOUR

It both irritated and impressed me that Dr. Kessler was right. Not only did the logistics of nights work well for me but I found myself falling into their flow as if I'd been born to it. I came to love that otherworldliness, the sense that we who worked there lived in the same place as everyone else but in our own dimension of it. More important, whatever happened on the surface of my life was subsumed by a much deeper satisfaction that I was more securely in this place I wanted to be, and that I found myself believing in the possibility of my future in a way I never quite had. Medicine had seemed a slightly fantastic dream, a thing to lust after but not quite to trust in the possibility of, as with a girl you knew was too good for you so that when she flirted you held something back in order not to be crushed when she ran away. Though I was taking a full load of classes now for the first time, I found myself doing well, the texts seeming to beam themselves into my brain. I'd come into a zone of concentration and focus I had never visited before. Old Dr. Masterson even called me into his office to congratulate me on how it was all going.

In the mornings when I came out I liked to stand on top of the parking garage and breathe. The night air was frigid now and the fetid fragrances of the city tamped down by it, and as the sun broke over the sagging houses outside the high fence and between the great brick buildings inside and came off all the thousands of panes of glass, I had to narrow my eyes. I often came off so hungry that my gut hurt as if I'd been punched or was sick. Sometimes I joined others at the Sunshine Diner for the breakfast platters or went out with Ray; often I went somewhere by myself and had only fruit and oatmeal and cigarettes; some mornings I went to Jerry Sobecki's on Monroe just where it came into the downtown. It was one of the rare decent places open that early and was always nearly empty then except for the odd wino or some autoworkers when the AMC plant was running a third shift, or sometimes a few from the hospital, people I knew well enough to nod at but not to want to drink with. Once or twice in the beginning they waved for me to join them but soon they stopped. I sat alone at the bar and sipped from the small eight-ounce bottles of Little Kings, intent only on the flavor and the intense coldness and the burn and rush of the cigarettes and of Jerry or his fat wife, Estelle, reading the morning paper behind the bar, waiting for someone to need something and the smoothness of the wood and the darkness and quiet and the low pleasant stench of that old place.

The workday sunlight and empty house I woke into later on the weekdays I didn't have early classes felt like a place I'd only come to visit yet I found some peace there. I began to walk through the tight neighborhoods in the afternoons, then to run—I'd once been a halfback and a sprinter; now I came to crave what opened in me only after a couple of miles. When you start, the legs ache and the chest burns from the cigarettes and the chilled air, but soon the muscles relax into that state of spring-like tension and the chest opens and deepens and finally the mind stops registering pain and begins to take in the world in a way that you otherwise feel only when you are stoned or in a city you've never seen before, when the sky is clear and hard and every detail, the faces of women and the shapes of buildings and the sounds of language and traffic, is exotic and beautiful and unspeakably fresh.

My nights off felt endless. I went out sometimes on the weekends with other students or a few times with hospital people, I studied and read novels, I watched television until I couldn't stand it, I lifted the basement weights Brigman had long ago stopped using. Sometimes I sat at the window in my bedroom and peered through the telescope Sandy bought me when I turned twelve (back when my scientific curiosities went beyond the human body to encompass the heavens) into the houses on the next street or into the three-story apartment houses that rose beyond them. I might sit for more than an hour waiting for that flash. I never saw anything of real consequence or carnal value but it didn't require that; a glimpse was all it took, a man stepping to the window to lower the blinds before getting into bed with his wife, a high school girl bathing open-mouthed in the azure cast of her television, a woman sitting under a desk lamp chewing her pencil, turning it in her mouth. I closed my eyes then and grew harder and hummed to myself until I came in silent unsatisfying waves.

One night in the Med-Surg ICU I couldn't find a scheduled draw. It was a bed number I'd never seen in the main open ward where the critical lay separated from each other by green drapes. I found it finally—an isolation cubicle in the back, a room barely big enough to maneuver in. It was an old old woman, older than people I knew who'd died of old age years before. The birth date on the work order, 7/23/78, had confused me, since Peds had its own ICU on a different floor. The patient was a hundred.

She lay still, her dark skin glazed and creased, lips drawn back, eyes closed. I tied a tourniquet on her upper arm and felt at the antecubital. It was warm but nothing came up, no hint of venous turgidity. I touched her hand and then jerked away as if its coldness had burned me. I saw then that she was too still. A handwritten note taped over the bed said NC in red letters—No Code. I felt up along her arm and found the line of demarcation midway between her wrist and elbow, the point to which the heat of life had receded.

A nurse stepped in. She wore green scrubs and over them a blue cotton smock. A red stethoscope hung around her neck. Something in her face went into me and I did not speak, neither of us spoke for a long moment. Then she looked at the woman and back at me and said, "Is she—?"

I nodded.

"I am so sorry," she said. She came over and rested her palm on the cooling forehead and brushed back the sparse white hair. Against it her hand with its high blue veins looked beautifully strong and vital. "Poor old dear," she said. "Are you new?" She glanced at my ID badge. "Daniel Redding?"

"Just to the night shift," I told her. "Call me Syd."

She was thirty-five anyway, I guessed, probably forty. Her rings, a fat diamond, a heavy gold band, an opal, hung from a safety pin on her smock. Her hair was streaked in blonds and blacks and layered back. She had hazel eyes and clear skin and a full and generous mouth, and she had that look that long pain brings, the kind you endure, whether it is physical or something else. I did not think she was quite beautiful. I had always liked the word handsome when I read it in a description of a woman, and wondered what sort of a real one it would fit. Here, I thought, was one.

"Don't tell me my husband chased you away."

And so I knew who she was—Ted Kessler's wife. It was right there on her own badge. I had seen her up here before, of course, on a few occasions, but hadn't made the connection.

I said, "Okay, I won't tell you."

She laughed and then in a gesture that felt both incongruous and endearing reached across the dead body, her hand open, palm up, beckoning. I wasn't sure what she wanted. I put out my own hand, and she grasped it and placed her other hand on top of it. I thought maybe we were going to pray.

"He does it to everyone, sooner or later," she said. "I'm Joyce. Welcome."

In the basement I set the tray on the counter in the office and washed my hands, which were trembling as they did when I let

myself get too hungry, though I had eaten not long before that. I
wrote "Cancel" on the order and tossed it on the table where
Phyllis was playing solitaire and eating a cheese sandwich.

She said, "What happened?"

"Dead."

She nodded and moved a card.

"She was a hundred."

"Hm," Phyllis said, never looking up.

In the lounge, Ray sat with his feet on the table. Oween, the
clerk, was at the sink, washing out the coffee pot.

I said, "That one was easy."

Oween sucked in her breath and said, "You talking 'bout that
old Mrs. Washington?"

I nodded.

"She pass?"

"Yes."

"Lord in heaven. Can you imagine?"

"I can," Ray said. "Dying is what old people do best."

"I'm talking 'bout havin to live on this earth for that long."
Oween opened a foil packet of coffee and poured it into the machine and closed it and turned it on. Taped to the machine was a
sign written on a paper towel that said: "Coffee ¢25, if you dont
pay this WILL be terminated." Someone had crossed out the word
"This" and written "You" over it.

I came home one weekday morning in that same gray season, a
time when the street should have been as quiet as the dead, to see
Donny bent under the hood of the Road Runner.

I'd always seen him as a stupid boy and later a stupid boy-man,
twenty-four going on fourteen who, if you told him you thought
down was a pretty direction, would jump. He'd been a year ahead
of me in school until the fourth grade, when he got held back. It
was a kind of attraction-repulsion dichotomy between us. Donny
was big early and I was not until much later, so the natural pro-

gression was that he thumped me around a little now and then, a well-timed shove that put me on my ass or a quick abdominal uppercut to short circuit my breathing. In retaliation, sometimes delayed for several days, I'd lay into him with my tongue ("Dim-witted dickhead!") and often as not make him cry before I left with a final epithet flung over my shoulder ("Fat-fuck flunker!"). It makes me cringe even now to remember the alliterative viciousness that came to me so naturally ("Repulsive reject! Reeking retard!"). Nothing he did to me could have hurt so much, and the sight of that big blotchy blob of a bully-boy blubbering tears and snot down over his lip, the fact that he had such a soft spot, that he could be so wounded after seeming almost animal-like, a product of nature's grosser forces, fascinated me.

I went inside and stopped in the living room before the stacks of magazines and papers and cardboard boxes and the filled ashtrays and the empty beer cans on Brigman's TV tray. I stood very still. The house should have been as quiet as the street but there was a noise in the kitchen, then Brigman came in holding a can of Schlitz. It could have been he'd called in sick or taken a vacation day but it wasn't. It went through me as a physical shock, another piece of evidence of the slippage of Brigman, which had been going on now for six years.

He was younger than Sandy by some years and never felt like Dad to me, even after they got married, nor do I think he wanted to. I couldn't go around calling him Step-Dad, so it'd just stayed Brigman and we'd spent much of our time together since then circling, grappling, I suppose, with the question of who we were to each other: competitors for Sandy's attention, friends, quasi-brothers, sometimes I guess even father and son. But there was no single word for it.

He said, "Hey, Little Syd." (My full name is Daniel Sydney Redding, in honor of my vanished blood father, Sandy's first brief husband, who was, I once pestered her into telling me, an Aussie.)

After the accident, though it must not have been easy, Sandy was able to cover us with her income. Nothing seemed to Chloe and me to change really except that Brigman wasn't there. When he got out, he didn't return to the plant and when he finally did take a part-time job at a small stamping shop at a fraction of his former wage he only held it for five months. Donny got him on at UPS after that; he stayed a year. Each subsequent job seemed to take him farther from what he knew how to do, which was to make machinery. He currently worked on the loading dock at a nearby IGA, but that was now apparently done, too, because they'd told him a week earlier that if he missed another day for whatever reason he was gone.

"You hungry?" he said. "I can do some eggs and pancakes. Coffee."

"I ate," I said, though I hadn't. "I've got class. Got to get some sleep."

He wore a white V-necked T-shirt and a pair of old green work trousers that sagged on him, and I saw in the morning light as I had not noticed somehow before how much his hair had thinned and lightened and that his several days' growth of beard looked thinner, too, and patchy. The skin on his red hands was flaked and cracked, and the flesh on his arms hung sadly. Before the accident he had always been about building up in whatever ways he could, but it took that away from him and now I could see, as if it had come suddenly, that he was an old man or near to it.

He looked happy to see me, though, as if this all happening in the morning instead of at night made it new somehow. He set the can down, took a pack of Marlboros from his pants pocket, and slipped one out. He held it pinched between his thumb and middle finger, the ember next to his palm, and said, "You doin' all right?"

"I'm all right, Brigman."

"Work and school, I mean. You holdin it together?"

"I always have."

"Not really."

"What do you want me to say?"

"Nothin. If you need some help—"

"You'll give it to me?"

"Try."

"With what?"

He watched as I went over to the staircase, then said, "Syd."

"Yeah?"

"It matters you do good at it and get out of here." He looked around at the dingy room full of trash and the dingy broken house, all the dingy houses on the dingy streets in this forgotten place. "I know it's been tough. Just do what you have to do, whatever it is."

The ceiling creaked. I looked up.

He said, "Chloe stayed home, too."

"Why?"

He exhaled and peered at me through the smoke, his eyes narrow and mean-looking as they sometimes got.

"She sick?" I said.

"No."

"What's going on?"

He shook his head. "Nothing. Everything's fine."

I went up and found her not in her room, which was next to mine at the rear of the house, but sitting on Brigman and Sandy's bed in the front, looking out at the street. Her nose was plugged, her face swollen from crying. I gathered there had been a fight.

"He didn't go to work," I said. "You know what that means?"

She nodded.

"How much has he had?"

"Not that much yet, I don't think. Couple cans."

"What happened?"

"He just treats me like such a baby." She continued to stare out the window as Donny crawled in under the dash to poke at something. "I want to get a job."

"What job?"

"A job job, for money. I have a friend who works at the mall, selling those hot pretzels. She said they need someone a couple nights a week and weekends."

"How you gonna get there?"

"You could drive me—"

"You can't count on that."

"Right. So, I was thinking I could drive Mom's car."

Sandy's '64 Buick Skylark hadn't been moved from our garage since the last time she drove it, in 1973, a few months before she died. The idea of the brand-newly licensed Chloe driving it now sort of shocked me, and yet it made sense—assuming we could get it running, why shouldn't she use it? Except that Brigman would never allow it. It was some holy thing with him, the last vestige of Sandy on the earth, a parked shrine out there covered in dust.

"So he said no."

"Like, *really* no. He got all pissed off."

"And what's Donny got to do with it? You all three didn't just happen to skip on the same day."

"He was gonna take me over to apply—the lady who owns it is only there during the day—but now Dad won't even let me do that. He told me I have to stay up here." Her face contorted and she squeezed her eyes shut as new tears came. The stain seemed almost to fluoresce when she got this upset. I had the urge to touch her, to feel her hair or the still little-girl-soft skin on the white side of her face, to try to smooth out somehow the confusion and anger that seemed so often to burn in her.

"I'll talk to him later," I said.

"It won't matter." She was right. It wasn't just the car. It was her going out to be exposed to the world in that way that he dreaded. But I was too tired to think about it. I went across and lay on my narrow bed and listened to Chloe start crying again and Brigman knocking around downstairs, and imagined I could hear Donny Tooman hammering out in the street.

Donny and Brigman had struck an odd sort of friendship when Donny and I were in our early teens, a kind of master and disciple thing when Brigman was still the Guru of Hot Rod and Donny would come over and help him work on his cars, and go with him sometimes to Motorhead. It was around that same time that Donny began baby-sitting for Chloe. She was maybe five, which would have made him thirteen. I don't know if it was so much a formal arrangement (I mean I could have sat for her if Sandy and Brigman had really needed me to) as a matter of convenience and keeping everyone happy. Even at that age, Chloe seemed to have a need to get away from home, and Sandy and Brigman seemed happy enough letting her go. So Sandy would phone across the street and Donny would come out to the berm and wait for Chloe to cross over. She was gone sometimes for hours over there. I was somehow aware that Brigman slipped Donny a wad of cash now and then to cover his time, though I believe Donny would have done it regardless.

As I drifted off, an image wafted back from the day before. I met Dr. Kessler outside as I was leaving. He carried a box of Dunkin' Donuts in his good hand—snitch food. I was just going to say good morning but he stopped and looked at me seriously and said, "If you have trouble with Ray, let me know."

"Trouble?"

"He can be hot-headed and careless. I don't mean in his work. His work is fine. It's other things."

I didn't know what to say, but I nodded.

"Just stay in touch. Stop by sometimes."

"Okay," I said, and though I had no intention of turning into another one of his informants I could feel the pull of his vortex, the desire he seemed able to instill that made people want to please him, to be on his side, and the headiness of the power of having his ear.

He said, "So I hear you've gotten to know the wife."

"I have, yes."

"Well?"

I kept my expression as blank as I could.

He said, "What do you think?" Again, I had no idea how to respond. It seemed like another snitch question, a followup to his having asked me to keep an eye on her, but he said, "Isn't she something?"

This puzzled me, too, that it should matter to him what I thought of her, or perhaps I wasn't puzzled so much as just surprised, but then I thought it went back to that impulse I'd seen in him before, that she was a part of the package of his achievements he needed to have recognized by whoever had the capacity to appreciate them. But the fact is he was right—she *was* something. As it happened in the few weeks after I'd found her dead patient, Joyce made a point whenever I went up there of stopping to say hey or at least to throw me a broad smile. If I was eating dinner alone in the cafeteria when she came in for her nightly tea, she'd sit across from me to talk for a few minutes. She was nice to talk to and to look at, and I began timing my breaks to coincide with hers, which were on a fairly regular schedule as long as things on the unit were under control. She commented on it once, saying, "You must spend all your time up here. Every time I come down, here you are."

"I'm just lucky, I guess." She smiled and looked away and I could tell that my saying it had pleased her.

I was thinking of this, but all I said to Ted was, "She's nice, a nice person."

"She's certainly given you an A plus."

He studied me for another moment as if he were looking for something, then said, "Well, remember, keep me in the loop. It's important. I can be a help to you, Syd."

Then he offered me his hook. I took it as I would a hand, and even a day later, as I lay in bed, I could feel how strange it had seemed to hold something so cold and dead but that moved as a functioning part of a human body.

I rumbled out of the hospital one December morning in the 610, the Tubes cranked, white punks on dope, and passed another Datsun, a sleek black 280Z pulled over with its hood up. Two women stood beside it huddled into their long coats against the wind and the first traces of new snow it carried. I could see their faces. I looped around and pulled up behind them. The license plate read Path 2.

Joyce said, "Well, aren't you just what the doctor ordered."

"You all right?" I said.

"The light came on. I pulled over but it started smoking."

"You didn't turn it off?"

"Well, then I did."

"Hey, that was good thinking. Was it smoke or steam?"

"I don't know. Steam?"

"You probably didn't burn it up completely."

"Did you just stop to be sarcastic, or are you going to actually help us?"

"I suppose I could help."

"Not that I'm not very good at taking sarcasm. Loads of practice, you know. It's just that we have to be somewhere."

"I can give you a lift. But let me take a look, first."

"You don't have to, Syd, really. I can call triple A."

I got a rag and a blanket from my trunk. When I came back, she said, "I'm sorry. This is my daughter."

"Jessi," the girl said. "Hi." She wore little rectangular glasses that seemed to hold her tormented bangs out of her eyes.

"Syd works in daddy's lab," Joyce told her, then said to me, "She rode in with Ted so I could take her over to the U for an interview. Just as a backup, you know. She wants to go to Case. Isn't that right?" She reached up and pinched the girl's bangs between her extended fingers and flipped them back away from her eyes.

I wrapped the rag around the radiator cap and unscrewed it, and snatched my hand back as it hissed and popped. I looked in, then spread the blanket and lay down and stuck my head under.

"Syd," Joyce said, "I can have it towed."

I slid back out and stood up. "Cracked hose. Probably been leaking for a while. Duct tape'll hold it for now. I have some."

"Are you serious?"

"Sure." There was a gas station up at the corner. I said, "You can get some antifreeze there."

"Will it be safe?"

"Till you can get it fixed right."

She looked at her watch. "Can you do it in fifteen minutes?"

"If you go get the antifreeze. And some water."

"Really?"

"Really."

I walked back to my trunk and got a utility knife and the roll of tape. I found the jack in her trunk, raised the right front wheel, then slid under again. As I worked, I heard them come back, and my car open and close. I'd left it running. Then Joyce was squatting beside me. I could see her ankles and her coat and the back of her skirt heaped in folds around them, and a little ways up inside, into the darkness between her thighs.

"She got in your car, if that's all right. She's cold."

"Sure."

I ripped a strip of tape. The wind sang and shook the car, but it was strangely comfortable under there, sheltered and heated by the engine, and quiet. Joyce did not speak. And then I felt something on my thigh, above the knee, and looked down and saw that it was her hand. I finished the taping but continued to lie there. I closed my eyes and listened to the engine ticking as it cooled and felt her warmth and the slight pressure of her fingertips, and the stirrings of an erection, until she took it away.

After I filled the radiator and started the engine she said, "Amazing." Her face was flushed. Tiny beads of perspiration sparkled in the faint blond hairs over her lip.

"Because I put some tape on a hose?"

"Because here you are." She looked back toward my car, toward her daughter, then said, "I owe you a drink, at least. Do you ever go out?"

"Sure."

"What are you doing Thursday?"

"Nothing. I'm off."

"I'm working second, filling in. Some of us are supposed to go out after. Ever been to Krystal's?" It was the area's newest biggest disco, out on Route 3 south of the city.

"Once."

"Well, maybe I'll see you then."

"Maybe," I said.

She got in behind the wheel and Jessi came up and got in beside her. When I put my hand on the doorsill, Joyce placed hers over it. "Thank you so much," she said. I stood back as she drove off, and felt the dampness from her palm lingering still on the skin of my fingers.

PART TWO

Recently, photography has become almost as widely practiced an amusement as sex and dancing . . .

—SUSAN SONTAG,
On Photography (1977)

FIVE

It was twenty minutes from our house through the far south city and southward still until, after passing through a semirural truck-stop intersection of competing diner–gas stations and into the country, you came upon the incongruity of a neon-lighted building nailed down at the edge of a vast farm field, alone there fending off the night. Beneath the signs it was perfectly nondescript—rectangular, flat roofed, built of cinder block and painted brown. It could have been a warehouse, and as I thought about it I realized it probably once was. The deep gravel lot was lighted only near the building.

Past the bouncer and the cashier's stall you came in through a long dark hallway that emerged into one end of a single cavernous room. The newness of the place didn't save it from the usual tackiness, and it had already in its few months been impregnated with the permanent stenches of cheap cologne and stale smoke and beer. The centerpiece was a raised underlighted dance floor above which spun the requisite mirrored ball with colored spots and laser beams reflecting and refracting from it. It was surrounded by wide swathes of tables and chairs, and along the right-hand wall stretched a mammoth bar.

I sat there and had just finished my first beer when I saw her come in. She was alone. She wore a kelly green dress, knit so that it hung onto her everywhere it could. I wasn't the only one watching as she came along the bar. She sat beside me and fitted a slender cigarette between her lips and lit it, then squinted her eyes and exhaled at the ceiling and said, "I don't smoke, really."

"Just on special occasions."

"Something like that."

Joyce ordered a Black Russian and another Little Kings for me and laid a twenty on the bar. Her hair was a little ratty and puffed out from her shift, and the effect along with the streaking made her look wild. We sat drinking, not talking, until I said, "How's that gunshot?"

A flight'd come in the previous night, a married man who was discovered by his mistress in bed with yet another woman, a new girlfriend. The mistress had gotten hold of a .357 and tried to shoot his cock off. She missed it but hit both femoral arteries. Phyllis sent up twenty typed and crossed units before they got him stabilized and through surgery. How he hadn't bled out no one knew but he was a young man, strong and thick, and though he was still unconscious they said his EEG looked okay.

"Fine," she said. "Do you want to talk about that place?"

"Not really."

"It's just that I have so much of it when I'm there. And then again at home."

"What happened to the others?"

"Who?"

"You said some of you were going out after work."

"I guess they were too tired." She opened her purse and took out a tin box and opened it and removed a black and white pill, then offered the tin to me.

"What are they?"

"Quaaludes."

"I never tried one."

"They're fun. And you don't have to drink so much."

I swallowed one and we drank a moment before I said, "So what do you like to do?"

"What?"

"When you're not having so much of it at the hospital or at home, what do you really like?"

She laughed and put her hand on my forearm and said, "I don't think anyone's ever asked me that." She sipped from her glass and adjusted it on the mat so that it fit back into the wet circle it had made, and said, "I like to sail."

"You have one? A sailboat?"

"My brother-in-law. He's down in Coral Gables. Have you ever been out? No sound but the wind and the water. The boat lifting and falling. It's like flying. The sad thing is we only made it down once last year."

"You can't afford your own boat?"

"Oh, we have a power boat here at the harbor—forty-foot Chris-Craft with twin custom Mans. But sailing, I don't know enough about it, and god knows my husband doesn't. We'd buy it and then have to hire someone to take us out in it. So we wouldn't go."

"It's so sad."

"Shut up," she said and laughed and touched me again, this time on the front of my shirt. She rubbed the fabric between her fingers and then opened her hand and pressed it against my chest.

"You know what else I like?"

"What?"

"Dancing."

"Ah."

"You're not going to tell me you don't."

"Aren't I?"

I took off my sport coat and hung it over the stool and she took my hand and led me onto the floor. It was "Le Freak" by Chic. I felt silly, as I always did dancing, but as the beers and the pill spread through me and I watched her, I began to let myself go into it, let her pull me in, and at some point knew I didn't look silly anymore because Joyce moved so evocatively that she made us both attractive. I became now simply a reflection of her.

We grooved through "Dancing Queen" and "That's the Way (I

Like It)" before the set slowed into "How Deep Is Your Love" and she moved in so I could feel her breath on my neck. I put my hands on her hips and as we moved together she pressed into me until I felt my cock swell. She ran her hands up and down my arms and I let mine wander back from her hips to the top of her ass. As I rubbed her there I felt no line, no impression, and knew that she was wearing nothing beneath the dress. She put her arms around my neck and pulled me tightly to her, and I pressed my pubic mound into hers and felt her rhythm, her slight thrusting. She kissed my neck and my cheek, and my cock was hard against her. The song ended and she gave me a little kiss on the lips and led me back to the bar, then excused herself.

I could feel the pulse of the bass in my eyes now as if I had become a part of it. In the mirror behind the bar I watched the light from the spinning ball cascade down over the dancers and dapple their faces. When the reflected lasers, riding in on the rails of the Quaalude Express, struck my retinas, they seemed to pop in my head like little fireworks and left me blinded to anything but bleeding spreading patches of color.

She came back and sat close beside me. I looked at her until she looked back and smiled, then I looked away. I felt her fingers on my arm again. She leaned over and said, "It's okay." I nodded but I did not know what that meant.

"I'm really hot," she said, and took my hand off the bar and put it on her thigh. "Feel?"

"You are."

"I need ice."

I sat for a moment before I got it, then reached into her drink and took out a piece. When I touched it to her she jerked and gripped the bar with both hands, then turned toward me as I moved my hand in little circles above her knee.

Her legs were pressed tightly together and I could feel the water gathering there in the valley they formed. I got a fresh sliver and slid it along her leg. The burn must have increased as it moved up but she seemed to relax into it. She turned toward me and let her legs spread slightly so that the water ran down between them. I pushed up beneath the hem of her dress and higher still until she made a noise, a kind of exhaling, then turned away.

"I'm leaving," she said.

"What?"

"For Florida, I mean. We are."

"Oh."

"We'll be gone through the holidays. It's too hot in here. I need some air."

I put on my jacket and as we walked along the bar and down the hallway she held my arm. She got her coat and we went out into the moonlight, and the delicious night chill burned my wet neck and armpits. I lit us both cigarettes as we walked across the gravel lot toward the 280Z, which she'd parked far out away from the building.

I stopped and watched her. In that moment in the cold pale light on that gravel in that field I thought of the weight of her, of her experience, of her jadedness, of her damage, and I wanted terribly for her not to leave me there. I say this as if it came upon me suddenly, but it was not sudden. I had begun in some measure to care about her, to contemplate her, to invent her for myself, from that moment in the ICU when she took my hand.

She unlocked her car door and said, "Are you okay?"

I went over. My head felt light and the breath came hot and dry through my lips. She looked up at me. Her eyelids were heavy and her mouth open. I thought I knew what she did not.

She said, "Thank you, Syd. It was nice."

"Don't go yet."

"I have to."

I leaned into her and waited and felt her breath on my face coming as hard as mine, then opened my mouth against hers. She put her arms around me and I pushed her against the car and ground into her and she spread her legs a little to let that happen. She turned her face away and I kissed her neck.

"Oh," she said.

I pulled the coat away and bit her on top of her shoulder.

"Oh, god," she said. "Stop."

I stepped back.

She said, "I've got to go, sweetie," and got in and started the car and closed the door and threw me a smile. As she drove away I felt the aching already radiating up through my pelvis.

In the morning I came down to find Brigman as I usually did now watching television, but on this morning he looked up at me with such longing anticipation that I felt it like a slap and remembered only then in my exhaustion, my mind reeling with images of Joyce, her scents still fresh, that I'd promised to take him over to the east side to look at a Plymouth. He'd been with Donny already to see it once, though he had no money and besides he was an old GM man and had made a minor avocation out of bad-mouthing Donny's Road Runner. And this car, whatever Brigman did to it, would never out-muscle the Road Runner, but it had called out to him somehow. This was all of course notwithstanding the central facts that 1) he was looking at a hot rod at all after having committed lethal carnage with one and sworn off them forever and 2) that he had lost his license after the wreck and never tried to reinstate it. But he'd always liked to look, even after jail.

"Come on," I told him.

As I drove, he sipped from a can of beer and watched the wide seedy world flash past, and it seemed to make him happy, as odd things did in those days.

I said, "How's Chloe?"

"Okay, I guess. Why you asking me?"

"I was just thinking about her and Sandy's car."

"She was your mother. Why you call her Sandy?"

"I don't know. Why shouldn't Chloe drive it?"

He looked out the window. There was no good reason but that the thought of it ate at him and I didn't know if it was because of his desire to keep the car safe and locked away, or to keep Chloe that way.

"I don't know," he said.

"I'd help you get it ready," I said. "It'll take some work."

"Some," he said. "It's pretty clean. I drained the gas out back when, so it ain't gunked or nothin. Needs new rubber."

I nodded, surprised that he was even talking about it, then (stupidly) I pushed. "She really wants that job."

"She wants this, she wants that. What's this all about?"

"Why shouldn't she work? She's old enough."

"She's got school to worry about."

"We're talking about a couple nights a week."

"I don't care."

"She needs to do something. Learn how to work. It's time, don't you think?"

"You don't even know, Syd," he said. "You just—*fuck*."

He stared out the window, chewing on his teeth. A little later, he said, "So how's the job?"

"Fine."

"You like nights?"

"Yeah," I said. "I do."

As we came onto the High Level, the great suspension bridge over the river, he said, "There a guy there who's missing a hand?"

It crawled down my back when he said it and burrowed in and turned around a couple times in my stomach. "What?"

"A doctor. I remember an article in the paper when he first came on at St. V's, one of those profile things. While ago. You were a kid. He lost it in Korea."

"Ted Kessler?"

"I don't know. He missing a hand?"

"Yeah."

"You call him by his first name?"

"Not to his face."

"But you know him?"

"Pretty well."

"No shit."

"Why?"

"He was 1st Marines."

This had some significance to Brigman. He'd been himself a marine in the later 50s, wedged in between the wars, so he saw no real action, though he went to the Philippines, I knew, and Cuba. He was booted with a dishonorable discharge after only a year but once in the club I guess you were in forever.

"They were the first ones in over there. Talk about the Shit. And he had this rep, I guess, of being a real bad ass. He made major. He had this small platoon of guys who were as crazy as him. He could get them to do anything. And supposedly he carried this big knife and liked to whack gooks bare-handed. Quiet, you know."

"This was in the newspaper?"

"Not that part. A guy at the plant knew him. After that article came out we were talking, he said he was this stone killer. Now he does autopsies and shit, right?"

"Yes."

"See, it's like he got this fascination with death. Couldn't leave it alone even after he got back."

"That's bullshit."

"Fuck it is."

"Somebody at Hydramatic knew Ted Kessler?"

"This guy was in, too."

"Korea?"

"The Corps. I don't know if he was over there."

"So how'd he know him?"

"He knew of him. He heard shit."

"A guy knew someone who knew someone who knew someone."

"It was in the newspaper."

"But not about him killing people with his bare hands."

"Shit," he said, and looked out the window again.

I felt as frightened as he was angry, though not because of some stupid story he'd heard. It was crazy, what I'd done with Joyce. I had good grades and I knew I'd smoke the MCATs when the time came, but even so I wasn't the choicest med school applicant anymore. Twenty-three was getting old, I'd be utterly dependent on loans and grants and whatever else they could provide, and I had no connections, no doctors in the family circle making calls and buying drinks on my behalf. Ted could wash all of that away. Or he could shit can me.

Brigman tipped what was left of the beer into his mouth, set the can on the floor and said, "It's down here. Turn."

It was a tight little frame house, one corner of which was braced up by cinder blocks stacked on a sheet of plywood—the man was always home, I gathered, collecting government checks while his wife worked. Out back was a garden of weeds and a saddle-backed garage with half-raised doors that hadn't moved in years and three dogs that I could see and as many kids, and there slowly dissolving in the dirty snow this faded lemon yellow 'Cuda. It was a '71 340, not the bulkiest of the muscle cars but it had nice lines with its hiked-up rear end and the tight linear body that narrowed as it swept down to the grill. This one was beat, though; it made me tired to think of what it would take to bring it back.

Brigman walked around and pushed against it, opened it up and peered in. I could smell the must from where I stood.

"You keep lookin," the man said, "you should just buy it."

"Problem is," Brigman said, "I got nowhere to work. Too damn old for curb work."

The man looked around and took a deep breath and brought something up from inside his chest and gathered it for a moment in his mouth and then hocked it out onto the ground. "Work on it here, you want," he said.

"Where?"

"N'a garage." He pronounced it gay-rage.

It was stuffed with thirty years of shit, shit that flowed out of every opening it could find. It was an older cousin to our living room.

"How's that?" Brigman said.

"Clean it there, a space. 'Course it'd be some rent."

"Like what?"

The man shrugged. "Twenty-five a month."

"That include electric?"

The man pondered it a moment, then nodded.

"It's a good deal," I said, and Brigman glared at me. I knew better than to comment in front of the seller, but I never thought he was seriously negotiating. This was verboten stuff, the fix he had denied himself for six years.

"You take it?" the man said. I watched his fat ruddy whiskery face as he looked around at the grim landscape, the sagging power lines and broken roads and weedy lots and falling down houses and the socked-in sky sitting on top of it all like some sadistic god wrestler pinning the world yet again. He tried to show nothing, as if the whole matter bored him, as if Christmas wasn't looming, and almost succeeded. I could see, too, in Brigman's face how he ached to put his hands on that machine, to make something work again.

"Gotta see about the money," Brigman said. "Make sure if I can swing it." But he hadn't found a job (I doubted he'd looked) and besides he had no way of getting himself over here except the buses, which would take an hour each way with the downtown transfer. I still wasn't sure why we'd come except that look he got when he touched it made him seem in some way as he'd once been.

The man nodded. "Don't come back here and look no more," he said, "less if you're gonna buy it."

We were headed back the way we'd come when Brigman said, "You know how he lost his hand?"

"Ted? Yeah, he told me."

"Really?"

"I said I knew him pretty well."

"So how?"

"He cut it pretty bad and it turned gangrenous before he could get in and have it taken care of. They had to amputate it."

"That's not what I heard."

"Oh, well then, he must've been bullshitting me."

"I heard he was at Chosin Reservoir when the Chinese made their big counter. He was in a building that collapsed. His hand was caught under a bunch of debris and he was gonna be dead if he didn't get out so he cut it off. Himself. Took that knife he carried and hacked his own fucking hand off. And now you work for the guy. Weird, huh?"

"I don't know how you can believe that garbage."

"I believe it," he said. "He probably *was* bullshitting you. Those guys don't talk about shit, you know, unless you're one, too. Less you seen it. Ask him sometime if that's not how it really happened."

"I'm not going to ask him that."

"Take me down there. He'd tell me."

"Jesus," I said.

"Fucking gook-killing machine. Wasted dozens of them little bastards."

When we came off the bridge and I turned into the lot of a Big Boy, Brigman said, "What're you doing?"

"Can you find the monthly?"

He was quiet a moment, then said, "Yeah. Unemployment goes another six weeks, then I'll find something."

"And you'll be okay with this again?"

"I don't want to drive it. Just work on it."

"*I* get to drive it sometimes."

"Shit, boy, you can drive it all you want long's you don't race. You sure? You gotta have the dough for school, don't you?"

"I have enough for next semester. Almost. But there's one more thing."

He looked at me and shook his head in resignation.

I said, "Let's just get it going, see how it is. That's all. It's doing no good sitting there getting old."

"I don't want her getting in trouble with it, is all, racing all over hell, doing . . . stupid shit in it."

"It won't hurt to see if it runs."

He nodded. I looped around and headed back over the river again to the east. The man came down fifty on his ask and agreed to take twenty for the rent. We stayed nearly an hour after I wrote a check for the car and the first month, me watching while Brigman pored over the engine, and the man swearing and kicking at one of the garage doors, trying to get the sumbitch piece-a-shit crap heap bastard open.

SIX

Donny drove Chloe to the mall one afternoon that week before Christmas ostensibly to do some final shopping but we knew she was also going to apply at the pretzel shop. This happened without Brigman's blessing but also without his expressly forbidding it—Chloe had continued to bug him about it until he finally stopped reacting at all and she could take his lack of response, pro or con, as tacit permission.

In the meantime Brigman, true to his word and with an eye toward a Christmas deadline, began fussing with my mother's Skylark. In a day he had it coughing, and a day or two after that running pretty smoothly. Then he had me back it out and test drive it with him in the passenger seat. We stopped first to get new tires (which were my Christmas present to Chloe), then found a big empty parking lot where he could take it around. He immediately ordered us back home, tore the wheels off to do an entire brake job including new drums, and also dropped in a new clutch. Chloe flitted about like a mother bird—her face would pop up in a window, then she'd be on the stoop, then in the garage, then back in the house again. Donny wandered over at one point and poked his head under the hood. When, upon seeing the modest six-cylinder 225, he mentioned that he knew where we could pick up a small-block V-8 four-barrel 383 with a high performance shaft, Brigman turned to him and said something either profane or threatening enough that Donny turned red and left a minute later.

But seeing them even for a moment with their heads together under a hood made me feel dizzy with nostalgia and dread. It had once been their fraternity. Brigman must have been thirty already when Motorhead formed around him, but it was as if only then did he find the place in the world that fit him, and ironically it was never a place at all—Motorhead had to move to stay alive, so you never knew where it was going to be until it happened. They came, Brigman and the others, to breathe and boast and let themselves out of themselves to burn through the nights of the city. They lived there in a way they could not live in the other places of their lives because they knew that anything was possible—fires or gunshots or knifings, revelations, acquisitions, wrecks, of course, arrests, the discovery of solutions to intractable problems, love, or other disasters they could none of them envision—and these possibilities sharpened the air and made it come alive in a way I imagined nothing else ever had for any of them. The noise itself felt dangerous, the simultaneous revving of two or three dozen magnum engines, big and bored-out and retrofitted and chromed-up and super-charged, each one generating over 350 horses or it didn't count, and the searing of rubber that went along with it, and shouting and laughter, the screams of girls getting chased by boys who knew them some and wanted to know them better, and the pounding of rock and roll from amped up Tri-Ax's, and often enough that eerie rising and dying of police sirens coming in. The lights, too, had edges, headlights and dome lights and street lights and lighters and flashers and store lights if it was in a parking lot and fires burning in garbage cans if it wasn't.

I was thirteen the summer of my first Motorhead and remember it as little more than a swirl of images and sounds and especially scents—the air laced with the smell of raw leaded gasoline and of the exhaust fumes of leaded gasoline, of raw rubber and of burned rubber, of the heated fusion of oil and metal. It was the smell of an industrial land, the same category of scents that strikes you in the factories where transmissions and glass and springs and batteries and the thousands of minute pieces that hold vehicles together and allow them to run are synthesized and stamped and welded and cooled and stacked and boxed, or in a garage or a trucking warehouse or a machine shop where the parts are tooled to minute specifications so they will all fit as they're designed to do. Even today I can step into a certain sort of building and be immediately transported back to the high heat and unlimited possibilities of those lost nights, though I remember little of what actually went on there.

Brigman taped a red bow to the Skylark's hood and left it in the driveway for Chloe to find Christmas morning. We all went along for her first drive, Brigman riding shotgun and Donny and me in the backseat (the two of us farting around pretending to be scared for our lives until Brigman gave us a look). It was not an easy drive, that car, with its pre-synchro-mesh three-on-the-tree shifter, and I thought at first that maybe Brigman should have waited until Chloe had a little practice before putting in the new clutch. You could practically smell it smoking. But he was patient, remarkably so—I saw them out nearly every day even in the slush crawling around the block until, soon enough, she was cruising smoothly and in the new year he let her take it out for the first time alone (and stood in the front door watching and smoking the entire half hour she was gone).

One night in early January Phyllis had off, so Ray was acting supervisor and Kathy Rudner (with whom, remember, I'd been working a couple mornings a week on Organic—I'd pulled that A with her help the first semester and felt primed for the second) was pulling OT. She didn't like to work with Ray but needed the extra money for Christmas bills. She held down hematology and the blood bank and when it was slow dozed on the donor couch in the back, but it wasn't slow that night, it was a wild ride: a girl awake and blinking at us with her scalp torn cleanly and completely off by a windshield, a sickler in crisis, two infarcts, an OD, and a rule-out Reyes. And that was all prelude to the flight that brought in a nighttime janitor who'd gotten caught by the sleeve in a shredder. Word was he'd managed to reach his knife and cut through whatever flesh was left of his upper arm, the bone being broken through already, and that if he hadn't done that it would have taken him all the way in. It brought to mind Brigman's story about Ted, and later that would gnaw at me but then it didn't have time—I was tied up there for an hour while Kathy cranked out units of blood and Ray ran all the other tests, jogging back and forth between Chemistry and Hematology.

After that it slowed and I dozed until a code came down around four from the ICU. It was the janitor. The senior resident running it spoke his orders in a low calm voice—in the ICU at night everyone stayed pretty cool. I stood hands in pockets away from the foot of the bed, watching them compress the man's chest and pump the bag while someone squirted conductant on the paddles and rubbed them together. Even then I was conscious of that place around me, its order and cleanliness. When the resident placed the paddles on the man's chest and popped him, everyone paused a moment to watch the new green blip on the monitor.

"Hey, you." Joyce stood beside me. "How've you been?" Her skin was so dark that the lab coat she wore over her scrubs seemed to glow against it. It made me feel sick how good she looked.

"All right."

She looked up and put her hand on the back of my arm. "I was just worried. I wanted us to have a chance to talk . . . after. You know. But it's been so busy."

"It's all right," I said. "I'm a big boy."

"Yes," she said. "I noticed that." She squeezed me.

"Bloods," someone said, and they broke into motion again and I came into the circle of light and felt for a radial pulse.

"It's awfully thready," a nurse said. "Can you?"

It was there, a distant flowing, more a vibration than a pumping, but as long as I felt it at all, I knew. "It'll come," I said. "Just slow."

"Get it," said the resident.

I uncapped the needle of a gas syringe and aimed it into a gauze and shot out the excess heparin, then felt again. I pushed the needle in and felt it cut through gristle and flesh, adjusting it as it traveled toward that distant flow, that tiny tide. The blood that came was dark, the color of ripe black cherries, and hardly strong enough to push the plunger back, but it came.

"Damn," someone said.

I sheathed and unscrewed the needle and capped the syringe and pushed it down into the glass of ice someone handed me, and left. In the hallway Joyce leaned into the ice machine.

She said, "How's your morning look?"

"Pretty open."

"Buy you a drink?"

"Okay."

I watched her walk back toward the unit. She'd taken off the lab coat and I could see all the contours of her round and substantial ass moving beneath the thin cotton of the scrubs.

I took a booth at Sobecki's instead of my usual spot at the bar. I'd just lit a smoke when the door opened and the tocking of footsteps approached across the wooden floor. Joyce wore a white sweater, a denim skirt, navy stockings, and clogs with wooden soles. She slid in across from me and smiled and lit a cigarette.

"Special occasion," I said, and she smiled. She took the tin of Quaaludes out of her purse and swallowed one and offered them to me, but I shook my head. Later, after a couple of drinks, she said, "I don't need to sit in a bar all morning. Can we go somewhere else?"

We came out into the sunlight of the morning and crossed the small weed-cracked parking lot to the 280Z. She unlocked the door, then looked up at me. I stood close enough to smell the wintergreen breath mint she'd taken, and her perfume, which was sharp, not soft and floral at all but vivid and vexing. It reminded me of Halloween, all orange and black.

"Do you feel like another drink?"

"Sure."

"It's just I don't want to have more and drive. My house isn't far. We could go there."

I nodded.

"Follow me."

A library lay on one side of the cool dark foyer complete with a sliding ladder to reach the higher shelves, and an emerald parlor with a tall silver Christmas tree still up on the other. I'd never been in a house that smelled so clean, not the antiseptic smell of the hospital but more the absence of any odors at all with just the hint of some underlying scent, not of cleansers or air fresheners but of a kind of flower maybe that I had never smelled before or some spice I couldn't have named. The dark garland-laced walls of the central hallway were covered with rows of photographs in matching brass frames. One, taken onboard a large boat, was of a smiling Dr. Kessler, shirtless and tanned, with his arm around a ten-or-so-year-old Jessi, but almost all the rest of them seemed to be of Joyce. Joyce as a very young woman, maybe twenty, Joyce pregnant, Joyce graduating from nursing school, Joyce with Jessi as a baby, and so on.

We passed through a huge dining room with a wooden table long enough to nearly span it, and into a wide bright kitchen of new stainless steel appliances and a glass table in a glass alcove.

"Sit," she said and crossed to the refrigerator and opened it and leaned in. She was built nothing like the women I'd been with. She was substantial in ways they had not been, in the breasts and the shoulders and neck, in the pelvis and thighs, in the belly, yet there was a kind of lightness in the way she carried herself. In the inebriating warmth of the light falling through the wide window, it occurred to me how simple about it they were, Ted and Joyce, how ignorant the walls and luxuries they lived behind had made them. What did they know really of the world? He had fought in a war and been injured, I'd give him that, and she got her hands dirty caring for the dying, but beyond that they lived terribly sheltered privileged lives, the dirt of the street, the rawness of the world, alien to them, at most a long distant memory. But not to me. I knew it and was certain I was smarter about this than they could ever be.

She set two Heinekens on the table then turned a chair out and sat down so close to me that when I faced her our knees brushed. She put her hand on my thigh and said, "It's okay."

"Is it?" I said.

She got up and stood behind me and said, "You need to relax." She began to knead the muscles along my shoulders and in my neck, squeezing, then driving a knuckle in until a great warmth flowed to my head and I did not feel light there anymore. I grunted and leaned back so that my hair brushed her. I let my head fall until it rested against the cushion of her breasts and as she continued to knead I reached around and rubbed her leg. She tilted my face back and when she leaned over and smiled and touched the end of her nose to mine it released something in me— I felt suddenly calm and voracious; I stopped trembling, my breathing deepened and slowed and the tension ran out of my shoulders and back. I slid my fingers into her hair and pulled her forward and placed my mouth over hers and we kissed in that upside down manner until she pulled away and said, "Wait here."

I listened to her clogs on the wooden staircase and drank and looked out the wide window at the yard. Soon she came back down, held her hand out and said, "Come." She led me upstairs and back to what I thought was a small TV room until I realized it was only the antechamber to the master suite. It held a black leather sofa, two end tables, and a bookcase with a television on one shelf, a Betamax player on another, and a row of videotapes.

She stopped here and turned and threw her arms around my

neck and kissed me again. For a moment she was like a young girl giddy with excitement, then she stepped away and held out her hands. She pulled her sweater over her head, undid the skirt and let it drop, and slid the stockings down and took them off so that she wore nothing but a white bra and white panties cut high up on her hips. She walked backward, facing me, into the bedroom proper.

It was mammoth, this room, running the entire breadth of the house. The rear of the ceiling angled downward with the roofline and beneath that lowered part sat the bed, king-sized with a heavy gold spread. The walls were the yellow-green color of avocado flesh. Ted's bureau was nearest the door. Her dresser, wider and lower and with a huge mirror mounted over it, lay beyond it, the two of them separated by the entrance to a walk-in closet. Across from the foot of the bed, along the inside wall, stood a huge oak-colored armoire, with its doors slightly opened. At the far end was a separate grouping of furniture—a suite of ornate matching arm-chairs and love seats.

Joyce stepped onto the bed as if it were a stage. She reached back and unsnapped the bra and then came forward to let me lift it away. When her breasts fell into my hands I felt something click deep inside myself—they were not only large, these breasts, but denser than any I had ever held, with stretch marks along the bot-toms and tight puckered nipples, and I thought that I had never felt anything so soft and heavy at the same time. And it wasn't just her breasts I found as I touched her. It was her belly, soft like an old woman's and slightly protuberant and flaccid but substantial beneath, renitent. It was the heavy flesh that had just begun to loosen behind her arms or at the insides of her thighs, the skin at the small of her back, or her wide dimpled bottom. It all had the same velvety texture, the same gravity.

She got on her knees and I sucked a nipple into my mouth. As she held my head against her the sounds of her cooing and sighing came to me directly through the wall of her chest. I slid a hand up between her legs to the panties and rubbed her there as she moved

against it, and ran a finger inside the elastic and felt her thick matted hair all damp and hot and beneath that the swollen nub of her
clitoris and then the slick wide opening. Then she got off the bed
and rubbed her hands across me and as she began to undo my belt
she said, "I've been thinking about this."

"Me, too."

"Have you? About me?" She held me and spoke very softly
near my ear as if it were some secret between us.

"All the time. I can't sleep."

"About doing what to me?"

"Kissing you. Touching you."

"Is that all?" she said. "Don't you want to fuck me?"

"Yes."

"But you could have any girl you wanted."

"I want you, Joyce. I want to fuck you."

"How do you like to fuck a girl?"

"What do you mean?"

"Hard?"

"Sometimes."

"How else?"

"Slow."

"Mm, another excellent choice." She let the trousers fall and
lowered my shorts and pushed me back onto the bed. She slipped
off my shoes and socks and my pants, then crawled over me and
kissed me and unbuttoned my shirt. Her hand was warm and she
slid it inside and touched me in the center of my chest and then on
my nipples, rubbed each one (moving her thumb in quick circles)
until it stiffened, then pushed the shirt back and slid it off so that
I was exposed to her.

"There you are," she said. "Such a pretty picture."

SEVEN

Weeks passed in which Chloe heard nothing about the job, but she refused to call. It was early February when I came home from class one afternoon and saw her in Donny's Road Runner, him holding her, hugging her, actually. I stood on the porch and watched until I heard Brigman behind me. He was smoking and watching from the door again. When I asked what was up he just glared. It wasn't until dinner (Church's Chicken on paper plates in front of the TV), at which Donny ate Chloe's share because she was upstairs in her room sobbing, that Brigman, several beers looser, his mouth full, said, "Hope you're happy."

"About what?"

"Didn't get the job," said Donny. " 'Cause of her face."

I looked at him.

He nodded.

"You see?" said Brigman.

I went up and sat on her bed but she wouldn't look at me.

"What'd she say?"

She turned just enough for me to hear her and said, "Go away."

"Chloe. Tell me."

"I don't want to talk about it."

"Well, I do. I need to know."

"Why do you need to?"

"I just do."

She sniffed and turned her face a little more. "She said people wouldn't want to buy food from someone who looked like me."

"Look." When she did I saw blood-crusted welts where she'd gouged the stain. "Someone like that is an asshole," I said, "a fool. You can't listen to that shit." But of course she did listen, and had been listening all her life.

It was only then that it struck me how much I had wanted her to get it, to begin to do something constructive in the world.

Weeks passed, too, after my morning with Joyce in which I awoke every day with my stomach knotted by concurrent emotions— self-loathing and disbelief at the carelessness with which I might have thrown away my nascent career, and fear that it would not happen with her again.

It was hard to tell. When I saw her at work she always smiled, and we talked and sometimes ate together as we had before. But she made no mention of our moment, not even a passing reference to there being anything like a relationship, an affair, going on be- tween us. Until one night I ran into her in the cafeteria, and she leaned into me and said, "Can you come over this morning?"

The first time had been furious and fast, a voracious alcohol- fueled muscle-fuck of the simplest sort. This time (though I would have been happy enough with what we'd had before) she seemed to want to linger over each moment, to manage it almost, to savor it, suckle it. She insisted on undressing me one slow peeled-off piece at a time, then positioned me crosswise on the bed and be- gan kissing me, on the mouth at first, lifting up and lowering her- self again and again as if I were a fountain she was drinking from, and then my chin and throat and down over my chest and belly. When she got there she lifted my cock and regarded it (eyebrows furrowed, mouth pursed), blew on it, then crouched between my legs and rubbed it over her forehead and her eyes and her cheeks before taking it in.

The few times I'd had it before were tentative and faltering and begrudging and incomplete and marred by teeth and thin lips, but this, the fullness and heat of it, the incongruity of the pressure of her tongue and lips and the roof of her mouth juxtaposed against the pull of the vacuum she created with her slight sucking, the unending wetness, was like nothing I'd felt. What was more she seemed to relish it. As if I were somehow working on her at the same time, as if my imminent orgasm was magically causing her own, she made more noise than I did. It did not last long before I called out and thrust into her, the pumping and emptying seeming to go on longer than I had anything to give.

She kissed up along my hip then and came to lie with her head against me, breathing as hard as I was and in the same rhythm, as if she were taking air from the rising and falling of my belly. After a moment, though, she got up and as she had the first time went to the armoire (which stood slightly open), slipped her arm in and brought out the short silk robe, shut the door tightly and went into the bathroom. When she came back she lay with her head on my arm and we were still.

After a little while, she said, "Do you think I hate him?"

"I don't know. Do you?"

"No."

"Oh."

"What's the matter?"

"Us," I said.

"Why?"

"I mean me. Why am I doing this?"

"Don't worry, Daniel." She'd taken to calling me that in private.

"You don't think he could blackball me?"

"I suppose he could find ways."

"Shit."

"Daniel. Listen to me—it's okay."

"You always say that."

"Do I? Well, I must think you worry too much." I remembered that he'd said that, or something very like it, once, too.

Outside a flurry of new blown snow batted against the window. The sky was low and heavy, and so it was dark there in the doctor's house and we dozed. When we awoke she smiled at me, and I kissed her. At first she seemed distant, tight and preoccupied as if she were going to get up, as if it were time for me to leave, but I kept on until she relaxed into it. We made love carefully this time, with her on top and my arms wrapped around her, and when she came she simply put her face into my neck and gave a single quiet cry. I held her against me for a long time, and we were still again, listening to the wind and the house and each to the breathing of the other.

Only a night or two later I heard Phyllis and Oween sniping about the pathology conference in Vail Dr. Kessler had jetted off to that afternoon, just in time for some late-season skiing. At first a delirious wave of hope washed over me, carrying images of the two of us, Joyce and Syd, together alone for a week. But the more I thought, the more I knew better, and when in the ICU I overheard one nurse say to another, "Must be nice, no notice. Just fly off skiing whenever you want," I knew Joyce had gone, too. It seemed odd that she wouldn't have mentioned it, but I didn't think about it much. It was during this time that I was to learn, or to hear at least, a couple of things that shocked me and began, I can see now, or at least marked, all the changes that were to come in our lives.

The first came at home. I was watching TV with Brigman, waiting for it to be time to leave for work. He was pretty hammered, having just finished a sixer. Chloe was upstairs—she'd taken to spending more and more of her time in the weeks since the pretzel debacle either cloistered in her room or across the street at Donny's house, her long-time refuge from the strains of her life. It was dark but for the luminescent screen that lit Brigman's face and the smoke that filled his opened mouth because he'd forgotten to exhale again. His eyes shined as he stared at Mary Hartman's rerun pigtails and bangs (she turned him on, I think). When Mary said something stupid but smart Brigman cackled and phlegm cracked down in his throat and set him off into a round of cigarette coughing. Then the front door opened and Donny came in with a rush of cold air and said, "Heya."

Under his breath but loudly enough for us both to hear, Brigman said, "Fuck."

I didn't know what was up, but Donny just turned and slipped back outside without a word. Brigman mumbled something that sounded like "Asshole," but I didn't ask him to elaborate. A second later Chloe came down.

She said, "Thought I heard the door."

"It was Donny. Brigman swore at him and he left."

"Shit."

"Watch your mouth," said Brigman.

Now, after a six-pack, was the time to keep quiet, to let it lie. She knew that, but she had been changing for a long time, since junior high really, toughening up, growing flip and nasty and careless, and it made me sad. I did not like to think about what she did with the boys she hung out with, though I knew. I had overheard her once on the telephone, a couple years earlier, talking to another girl with the sort of candid frankness, the carnal familiarity, that I knew older women had with each other but which shocked me to hear from a girl. And it was not speculative talk but a kind of comparing of notes, of how far, of where, of what hurt after. Brigman got regular calls from school about her attitude or something she had been caught doing—smoking in a john or making out in an empty classroom or being dressed inappropriately. But there in the dimness in the face of Brigman's silly admonition, when I watched her cross her eyes and look down across her nose and push her lips way out so she could see them and say, "Shhhit," I laughed.

"He ain't comin in here," Brigman said. I gathered this was still about Donny.

"Fine," she spat back.

"What the hell—" I said.

"Stay out of it," Brigman told me, and Chloe said, "Syd," and shook her head and came over and sat on the arm of my chair. It was a commercial now for Alka Seltzer (he couldn't believe he ate the whole thing).

"I mean it," Brigman said to her.

"All *right*," she said. "Jesus. Drop it."

"No, *you* drop it, Little Miss Jailbait."

"God—"

"What *is* this?" I said.

"Ask her," he said, "what she does with him over there."

"Just stop it," she said.

"What she's *been* doing with him, I'd like to know for how long. Good ol' Mr. Baby-sitter."

Chloe stood and pointed at him and said, "Don't you say that. Don't you *ever*."

"It's true, ain't it? What were you, twelve when it started? Thirteen?"

"Brigman, come on—" I said.

"*Ask* her."

But it scared me in that moment that he was telling the truth or some version of it—that Chloe and Donny had begun something together and that maybe it went back between them to when she was a little girl. It would never have occurred to me, Chloe and Donny in that way. They'd always had this weird bond (he was the one she went to as if even as a young child she sensed who it was would stick around—these parents might fall away but Donny would always live across the street). And it suddenly made a certain sick sense that something more than that had grown between them. Maybe that's even where it had started with her, in those unprotected years with Sandy dead and Brigman lost in his grief and his beer. I felt dizzy and nauseous.

The door opened again and Donny stood there holding up a six of Blatz like it was a trophy and he was the champion of something. I tensed but all Brigman said was, "Piss water."

But when Donny came in and held it out to him, Brigman, after hesitating a moment, pretending to consider it, pretending that he might refuse it and kick Donny out, of course accepted it and tore off a can for himself and one for Donny. What a scheme! I knew Donny could sometimes be perceptive for a stupid shit, and of course he knew how things worked (that with six down Brigman could get damn mean, but a few beyond that would put him out cold until morning), but this guile, this blatant manipulation, was nothing I'd have thought him capable of.

"You ain't hangin out here," Brigman said.

"Just come over to say hey."

He looked at Chloe and I saw something pass between them, then she went upstairs. After he finished the beer, Donny said, "Well, take it easy," and left as well. *Mary Hartman* was over. By the time the early news came on, and I had to leave, Brigman was snoring in his chair. Chloe stepped around the wall from the staircase. She'd changed into fresh jeans and a nice blouse, and I smelled Charlie, the perfume she wore. She opened one of the remaining cans of Blatz and squeezed into the big easy chair alongside me, our hips mashed together, and said, "He wants it so bad for you."

"Who?"

"Brigman, stupid." She sipped and handed the can to me. "You don't know how much. Doctor Syd."

A sudden tide of regret flooded through me. We were both, my sister and I, fuck-ups in a literal sense—we were fucking our lives away. And at that moment I cared less about mine than I did about hers. I wanted so terribly for her to have something decent and normal, a real job, a healthy family. Nothing spectacular. Just to learn how to live in the world without destroying herself out of some kind of self-loathing. I wanted her to sell goddamn pretzels at the mall, to wear the little jacket and hairnet and get a paycheck every week, and to come home and not go out and ride around in cars and drink and give blowjobs to pimply little shits who cared not a whit about anything beyond her body and what she could do with it. And maybe to go to college but even if not to make enough to live in a good place and not always be scraping for everything she needed. Though perhaps I had gone a long way toward ruining that possibility, too. Because if I got into medical school, found entrée to that life, surely I could pull her up with me. I was fucking it up as surely as she was. Beyond that, I had thought about what other consequences my sinning might lead to—this was a long-standing marriage I'd tampered with. Maybe what was really frightening was the danger I saw in me, not of action but its opposite, of just letting things carry on until it was too late to save anything.

Chloe took another slug from the can, then pried herself up and went to the front door and looked at me, waiting it almost seemed for me to say something. When I didn't, she said, "Night, Little Syd," and was gone.

The other thing I heard at work. Ray and I were pounding coffee in the lounge and playing two-handed euchre, waiting for something to happen. Oween stood at the sink washing the pot. Ray said, "Shelley says we should go out. Us and you and you bring someone." They had no kids with both of them past thirty, a nearly paid-off house, new twin Fords every couple years, and another thirty or forty years of it looking Ray in the face. When we drank in the mornings, I often had to pour him into the car to get him home.

"Who'm I supposed to bring?" I said.

"I don't care. Find somebody. Bring Oween."

"Uh-oh," she said, "don't you be draggin me in on this."

"She's married," I said.

"You wouldn't let that stop you, would you?" Ray asked her.

"Ain't sayin nothin about nothin. Just go on about my *own* business. Mm." She shook her head and left.

I put a card down and said, "Do you let it?"

"What?"

"Being married, stop you from screwing around?"

"I did all that. That's why you gotta wait."

"Who would it take for you to do it? Like say you're home alone and Farrah Fawcett-Majors knocks on the door."

"Fuck Farrah Fawcett-Majors."

"Would you?"

"Too skinny."

"There's got to be someone. Jane Fonda."

"Fuck Jane Fonda."

"Linda Ronstadt. Carrie Fisher."

"Cybill Shepherd."

"Yeah?"

"I'd let her blow me."

"Who else?"

"I'd let Kessler's wife blow me, too."

"What?"

"The nurse. What's her name. Joyce? She'd do it, too."

"What do you mean?"

"I mean she'd blow me."

"In your dreams, maybe."

"Listen—Shelley and me were at Krystal's. She goes to the head. I'm walking around, I see Joyce at the bar. Alone. I say hi and she starts coming on—hard. She was pretty tanked and she had that fuck-me look, you know. I mean, she was ready."

"When was this?"

"Two, three weeks ago. She's touching me and talking about shit, what a big guy I am and we should get together sometime. I mean, goddamn, if Shelley wasn't there . . . Later, I seen her with some other guy. He was gettin' some of that."

"It wasn't Ted?"

"Fuck no. She doesn't sleep with that asshole. I heard she fucks like half the new residents every year."

"That's bullshit."

"She got to get it somewhere."

"And how do you know all this?"

"I hear shit. Look, she wants to work, fine, but why nights? She needs the shift differential? It's cover so when she wants a night out there's no questions."

I didn't know what to make of Ray's story, whether I believed anything about what he thought he saw. But just the image of it, her with other men, although I'd only ever been with her twice in that way myself, gave me pains. The larger issue, of course, was school—Ted helping me, me helping Chloe, our helping Brigman, and all of us getting pulled up in the world—not throwing that possibility away for the chance to sleep with a doctor's wife, however attractive she was to me, however much I found myself dreaming of being with her again. So it happened that I came to decide that it was time to stop.

EIGHT

I was sitting on the counter in Chemistry watching Ray spin down the last batches of the night when Ted walked in. It was early, barely past six, and he looked beat-up, puffy and red-eyed and saggy, but it was his first day back after the conference-ski trip. He glared at me and said, "Get down from there. Don't you have work to do?"

I shook my head. I could feel my heart.

"That lounge is a dump," he said to Ray. "Newspapers. Dirty plates. What do you think it is here?"

Ray shut off the centrifuge. "It's just been a long night."

"You were in charge, Ray. You're responsible. How do you think it looks, a mess like that? In a laboratory?"

"I'll take care of it," I said.

Barb Lancioni was in the lounge making fresh coffee. When I came in her mouth fell open, its motors kicking in, but I had already set in to picking up and she seemed to sense that it would be better not to speak just then. She restricted herself to clicking and humphing and sighing as I stacked plates and cups in the sink and put in soap and filled it. I wiped down the table and cupboards and put the food away, and had begun to gather up newspapers when Ted came in. Barb glanced at him and hurried out.

He said, "I warned you about him. He's careless. He'll get you in trouble. I don't like when he's in charge."

"The work gets done."

"Did you and Kathy have a chance to study?"

"No. It really was crazy."

He sat on the love seat and leaned forward and pressed his palm against his forehead as if he were sick or in heavy thought.

Joyce had worked that night. It was the first time I'd seen her since they left. I wanted to talk and so, apparently, did she, because when I first came up to the floor she told me I was meeting her in the morning at Piasecki's. It was not a request.

"Dr. Kessler—"

"Be quiet, Syd."

"Can I—"

"Ah!" he said and waved his hook toward me as one might wave a hand to cut someone off, but if you'd been watching with the sound off I think it would have looked for all the world as if he were slashing at me.

I leaned against the counter to wait until he was over his crisis or whatever it was but he finally just said, "Go," and so I did. Barb had lingered in the hallway to listen and I surprised her. Though I said nothing, made no gesture, she blanched and stepped away from me.

On our way out to the parking garage, Ray said, "Ted the Head. What a dick. Married to a piece of ass like that and lets her work the night shift. Grab a brewski?"

"Nah," I said. "Not today."

We only got through one drink before she said, "Are you coming over, Daniel?"

"What do you mean?"

"You know what I mean. You're acting strangely. Like you don't want to be with me."

"No," I said. "I do—"

"But?"

"I don't know. It's . . . not right. It's crazy."

"Doesn't it feel right when we're together?"

I nodded.

"I like being with you very much. I want us to be more."

"But, Joyce—"

"I told you before not to worry. You don't understand everything about my life. It's not all what you think."

"What does that mean?"

"It means stop worrying about it. Please can we go home?" She got teary and picked up her purse and walked out. When I caught up to her in the parking lot, she said, "You drive," and got in my car. Before we were out of the lot, she had my trousers open. She lay across the seat with her head in my lap and took me hurriedly, deeply, greedily, as if it were a kind of nourishment she needed. A truck driver going the other way pulled his air horn. When I came the road wavered before me and I held it steady only by focusing on the yellow speedometer numbers and the solid white line at the edge of the asphalt, and that essential concentration made it somehow even more intense.

She went into the bathroom when we got there, so I walked upstairs alone. When Joyce came up, she carried a tray that held two glasses of ice water, a bottle of massage oil, and several clean white towels, and she was naked.

"What are you waiting for?" she said. As I undressed, she put the tray down and folded back the spread and the sheets and lay upon the bed.

"Come," she said and opened her arms. I tucked my face against her breasts and she held me and for a long time we lay without moving. When I looked up at her at last, she said, "I was afraid you didn't like me anymore."

"I could love you. That's the problem."

"Oh, Daniel." She looked away. It was the first time I remembered anything I said having flustered her.

I said, "Do you see anyone else, Joyce?"

"What do you mean?"

"Other men."

"Now?"

"Yes."

"Well, I have a husband."

"Besides him."

"Sleep with them you mean? Have sex?"

"Yes."

"No." She shook her head and smiled so sadly and sweetly that I felt it go clear through me. She touched my cheek and I turned my face into her hand and breathed in the smell. "Do you think about me with other men?"

"Sometimes," I said.

"Do you like it?"

"No. I don't know."

"It hurts, but it's exciting."

"Yes."

"I'd do that for you."

"What?"

"Be with another man."

"Do what with him?"

"Anything you want. As much or as little."

"God," I said. "Joyce."

"Is that something you're interested in?"

"I—I don't know."

"Are you ashamed of it? Of thinking about it?"

"I don't know. Yes. Maybe."

"Please don't be. We can talk about it. I can even whisper it to you. Do you know what I mean?"

I nodded.

"Anything is possible, Daniel. *Everything* is. Do you understand that?"

I did not. I did not.

She said, "Turn over," and sat on my bottom and with the oil wrote a slow S on my back. "I've been thinking so much about you," she said.

"Have you?"

"Yes."

"While you were skiing?"

"All the time."

The oil absorbed the heat of her hands and the friction of her rubbing and transferred it to my muscles. When she twisted her knuckles and drove them in, it went in more deeply still.

"I thought about you, too."

"What about?"

"How we should stop."

"Shh. Just relax. Just be, Daniel. Can you do that? Can you let the moment hold you? If you could learn that—"

She rubbed my neck and shoulders, my ass and my legs and feet and toes and each bit of webbing between the toes, and my arms and hands and fingers, and then she had me turn over and massaged my face and my chest, then my genitals, focusing not on my cock so much as my scrotum. She oiled it and warmed it in her hands, taking each testicle in turn and rolling it gently between her fingers, squeezing it slightly so that I felt the faintest aching.

When finally it was too much I had her lie face down and slipped a pillow beneath her hips and knelt behind her and in a single unbroken movement slid in. She exhaled and pressed her forehead against the mattress and said, "Oh, my Daniel." I moved slowly and watched the entering and the reemerging. Then I came out and lifted slightly and placed the tip against that puckered annular button.

She stopped moving and seemed to hold her breath, then she breathed and lowered her pelvis slightly and said, "Go." The greater resistance yielded only slowly at first with a delicious gradual sliding and parting, and then abruptly so that I found myself suddenly plunged in to mid-shaft. She cried out, in pain yes, but not only in pain, not only, and she talked to me, telling me to wait,

wait, then to go slowly, slowly, but not to stop. I pressed further into that hot cloud; that's all I could think of, I was fucking her cloud, fucking her, fucked her, hurt her, I hated her, I loved her, I understood nothing about her, not what she wanted, not what she loved, not what she dreamed about, not what she hoped and waited for, not what mattered to her, nothing except that she'd told me anything was possible, everything was, and I did not see how that could be but I wanted it to be, I wanted it so much. That's all I wanted: everything.

Later, as we lay together, I heard the distant sound of the doorbell chimes. She got up, and went into the dressing room to a side window that overlooked the driveway.

She said, "Shit."

"What is it?"

"UPS. Ted's been waiting for this package." She opened the window and called out, "Hold on!" and then went to her dresser and took something from it and came back across to the armoire. Her body blocked my view, but it took a moment for her to open it, as it would if she were unlocking it. She opened the door slightly and reached in and took out the red robe and closed it again and smiled at me and hurried downstairs.

I lay looking after her, then around the room. When my gaze fell across the armoire again it caught on something, a shadow where the two doors met, a certain gap—she had not closed it completely.

I stood and went over and pulled on the door and it opened, the catch that should have locked it snapping down. It took a moment to know what I was looking at—it did not fall into place at once but rather in a series of realizations, some minute, some astonishing, each linked to the subsequent one, a domino chain that fell rapidly, surely, inexorably backward from the moment in which I stood to the moment we'd met. I looked numbly dumbly at the machinery, the heavy Betamax recording deck mounted on a lower shelf, the thick cables running from it along the inner wall to the higher shelf, where the camera (a Sony, it declared in burnt orange letters) was mounted, its single bulbous eye staring, if blindly just then, out at me. At the room. At the bed.

I turned as she came in. She, too, was staring at me, my stricken expression reflected in her own.

"I don't understand."

"Daniel—"

"What is it?"

She looked as if she could not bear to see my face, that register-ing, the dawning of my knowledge of the betrayal, of the horrible breach she'd committed, continued to commit, against me.

I said, "What have you done?"

"Nothing, baby. Nothing now."

"Now?"

"It was over. Do you see? It's all different. Oh, my god, I'm so sorry."

"Who was it for?"

"Daniel—"

"Who was it for?"

"At first it was just for us. Him. And me." I waited. Tears fell from her chin onto her breasts but she did not seem aware of them. "And then—then it's what you were for, in the beginning. It's what made you possible. Made *us* possible. Can you under-stand that?"

I looked out the window. I felt vacant and curious. I said, "Who watched it?"

"Daniel, please—"

"Ted?"

"Yes."

"And you."

"Yes."

"Together?" I looked at her.

She nodded.

"Tell me one more thing."

"I'll tell you anything," she said.

"Were the tapes just foreplay? Or did you actually fuck him while you were watching?"

"Both."

My legs went suddenly numb and I fell to my knees. It felt as if I had been stabbed—a mingling of shock and incomprehensible pain and disbelief at the horror of it. Then I felt a crack, and as if I still extended to her, was still a part of her, it seemed to rend her, too. We fell together, she to her knees and I forward so that my face rested on the floor. I wailed, the breath rasping and tearing in my chest.

Now she crawled to me, to hold me, but I put my hand out violently to ward her off. She squatted, wanting I knew to touch me as much as a part of me still wanted her to. "I didn't want to! It was his idea. I just wanted you. It was wrong, but I wanted you so badly. And then I knew it had to stop. That's why I went with him to Colorado, to tell him—"

"Fuck what you told him."

"—about us. About you and me. That I didn't want to play anymore. I just wanted to be with you."

"To play?" I said. "At Krystal's that night, was he there, too?" She nodded.

"And after you left, you went and fucked him." He watched. That was their game, their foreplay. Only with me it had graduated to something new, something they could keep and watch over and over again, together. I reached up and gripped the top of the armoire and pulled with my full weight against it until it leaned and teetered. I leapt back as it fell with a tremendous splintering crash. She did not move.

I said, "Where are the tapes. I want them."

"Gone."

"You're such a mother*fucking* liar!"

She sat up. She shook her head. She said, "It's true."

"Where?"

"They're erased, Daniel."

I rushed out into the anteroom, to the row of tapes on the shelf above the video player and began madly pulling them out, looking at the labels, tossing them aside. I tried to fit one into the machine, tried to turn it on, then let out a gurgling cry of rage and yanked the television set off the shelf. It imploded when it landed, and a faint cloud—of fine glass dust perhaps or of the shadows of images—rose around it. I leaned forward, placed my hands on my knees and began to gag, great heaving spasms that rolled up from my lungs and stomach racking me until I vomited bile.

Now she stood again, now she came to me, to clean me, for she took off the robe as she came and wadded it up. But I straightened and put my hand on her bare chest and shoved. She stumbled backward and landed hard on her bottom.

I picked up the robe. I said, "You weren't modest. It was just so you had an excuse to lock the door, after." Even in that moment, that confusion, I wondered for how long I would have these little revelations, pieces snapping into place, moments recast.

I looked at her and said, "I didn't mean for you to fall."

"It's fine, Daniel."

I hurried back into the bedroom and dressed. She pulled herself up and leaned against the doorframe and watched me until I shoved past her and started down the stairs, then limped after, calling out, "Daniel! Wait! Please! You need to talk. You need to listen. You'll hurt yourself like this!"

She chased me downstairs, and when I tore open the front door and went out she followed me still and stood on the walkway, stooped forward, knees pressed together, hugging herself. I backed so hard down the driveway that I veered and slid off into the yard, and when I pulled forward the wheels threw up dirt and grass and left ugly black furrows on the lawn.

As if her nakedness belonged to someone else, she remained there on the walkway, and I would later imagine her in that way— exposed in front of a doctor's great house in the estate section, looking around at the neighbors and at the road again as if there might be someone still somewhere who cared to look back at her.

PART THREE

Fuck this and fuck that
Fuck it all and fuck the fucking brat

—THE SEX PISTOLS (1977)

NINE

It was a small school of the wealthy and when, on the Monday after her party, in front of her fellow students, Jessi Kessler climbed into this raw-looking muscle car driven by some new guy, blooms of satisfaction rose in her white cheeks. Kids swarmed around looking in and some of the boys gave thumbs up or raised their fists. When a bloat-bellied man in a suit stepped outside to watch (the buttons of his vest nearly hopping off into space), I did not light it up, did not so much as rev it, but even at a crawling idle the 'Cuda sounded dangerous, each percussive burst discrete and sharp and amplified by the new glass packs Brigman had put on. You knew just from listening what lay beneath.

"So how're the folks?" I said.

"Not back yet. Some flight thing. They'll be in today."

Do they know? I was itching to ask. Did you tell them?

For someone who claimed to disdain her classmates she seemed awfully preoccupied with them. I nodded and glanced over now and then into the stream of her nervous yakking while holding out before myself (envisioning it there on the road ahead) that moment when it dawned on the Two Shits who their daughter was hanging out with, and the delicious possibilities beyond that. We drove south and then east into the city and it wasn't until we were at the edge of the downtown that I realized she'd shut up.

"You okay?"

"Where're we going?"

"Nowhere."

"Can we go over the bridge?"

I turned on to Broadway, then the on-ramp.

"I like to think about it," she said.

"The bridge?"

"Well, the river. Water. If you were going to commit suicide, how would you do it? I mean, you know, theoretically."

There was a pull-out up at the top that I think was for emergencies but I stopped so we could look out at the city, in one direction the buildings and street-maze of the downtown and in the other the old loading docks and elevators and warehouses along the shoreline.

"It's so beautiful," she said.

It wasn't at all really except to an odd eye but I had one, too, had often wondered if it was only me who took so much pleasure in the grimy worn-out soot-stained vistas of my childhood, who loved, too, the bouquet of that burned air, who felt regaled by the raucous sounds of artificiality, of the man-made. A strange girl, I thought, strangely attuned.

I said, "I don't think about it."

"But if you did."

"I don't know."

"They say guys usually do it fast and violent. Shoot themselves in the head or crash into a tree or something. And girls do it quiet, like pills or whatever."

"Is that what you'd do?"

"I'd jump."

"From here."

"Yep."

"Why?"

"I've heard drowning is supposed to be cool."

"Oh, yeah?"

"Not painful at all—you see colors and like go outside yourself."

"I wonder how they know that. I mean, who'd they interview?"

She didn't respond.

"You'd probably be killed, anyway," I said, "or at least knocked out when you hit."

She looked away from me, out over the water.

I said, "I guess it would depend on how you hit. I mean, if you hit feet first maybe you'd stay conscious so you could enjoy the drowning."

"We don't have to talk about it anymore."

I drove down into the east side, and past the refineries and the rings of neighborhoods and small plants into the far countryside where it was a flat even mile between each intersection.

"Hey," I said, "mind if I stretch it out a little?" I was anxious to see what Brigman had wrought.

She nodded but looked pale.

"You sure?"

She shrugged.

I turned onto a desolate stretch and stopped and then put it down. The blacktop was warm, so the tires gripped like they had teeth and you felt the back end lurch then hold and the front end lift as your brain settled back in its pan. The sensations—the Gs, a raw high scream of explosion and compression, a shuddering of dash and doors, a wafting of fuel—piled up as I wound out each gear, watching the tach, punching the clutch, every shift bringing a bark of the tires on the soft asphalt (which said all you needed to know about what Brigman had done to the back end). We'd just hit one-thirty, the next intersection rising up, when something in front let go. It was a tiny tock, a brittle snapping that I felt as much as heard but enough to send the car listing heavily to the right. At a normal speed it would've been no crisis but over a hundred if I put so much as the edge of a tire off the road we'd've rolled a dozen times. As I fought it (arms vibrating) and braked (so that now the pressure flew forward into our eyes) the right tires touched the berm and sent a swarm of pebbles clattering up against the door and the underbody. Jessi screamed. I leaned and pulled and braked and gritted my teeth and the tires caught and we came back and I was careful or dumb-lucky enough not to overcorrect and send us off the other side and we came to a hard squealing stop.

"Did you hear it?" I said, mostly, I suppose, to make the point that something had gone wrong mechanically, that it wasn't just my bad driving. She opened the door and I thought she was going to get out and walk the twenty-five miles home in justified anger, but she leaned forward between her knees and threw up. I found some cleanish rags in the trunk to give her.

"I'm sorry—" I began, but she shook her head.

"I just get motion sick sometimes."

"I mean—something let loose. In the suspension."

She nodded. We sat until she seemed to breathe a little easier and a bit of color came up in her face, then I drove us back. The something clicked now in the right wheel, caught and released with a shearing sound, and I drove tensed against it. Jessi sat with her head back, eyes closed, breathing through her nose, and it occurred to me that it was maybe the end already, that I had ruined Brigman's car and my beautiful plan of reprisal all in one careless moment. By the time we passed beneath the trees on her street she'd gone pale again—forehead damp, hands trembling, blouse matted with sweat. I caught her faint sour scent. Ted's BMW sat in the drive. When I said, cruelly, I suppose, "I still owe you that bite," she put her hand to her mouth and did not look at me. She opened the door and ran toward the house. I noticed a face in one of the upstairs windows.

In the early morning we got in a bad gunshot. There were so many people crowded around that I couldn't get in to do a draw (this notwithstanding the fact that the guy likely didn't have enough blood pressure for me to get anything, anyway), and Phyllis was waiting right there in the ER for anything she could use to do a type and cross and they could get off the O neg they were pumping in. So I crawled under the cart and scooped up some large clots for her to spin down. I had to wait around then for the docs to do a femoral stick for a blood gas, etc., so when I finally got down and dropped off my bloods it was well after seven, the day shift was in high gear, and Ted was standing in the hallway by his office. Waiting, apparently. He pointed at me.

"Sit down," he said when I came in, then shut the door and stood behind his leather chair, arms resting on its back. He seemed relaxed except that his lips were white. He said, "What happened?"

"Guy got shot." I had blood all over my corduroys and shoes and lab coat.

"You know what I mean. You broke the rules, didn't you?"

"Rules?"

He regarded me for a long and uncomfortable moment, then said, "I know about it."

"It was an accident."

"An accident?"

"The—what are we talking about?"

"You have no business doing anything with my daughter. None. Let alone making her sick."

Well, sick, yes, I thought, but I also almost killed her. Did she happen not to mention that? "So she told you—"

"She didn't tell me anything. I heard her come in retching. I saw the car backing out and got to some binoculars and read the license."

"You had it traced?"

"Yes."

I was impressed with this and also cognizant of the real importance of what he was saying—that his oh-so-bright and alienated seventeen-year-old had said nothing about me or what had happened, and that this could be interpreted as her protecting me, shielding me from their wrath. Or just that she hated them and didn't really tell them anything at all of her life.

I said, "Wow."

He nodded (almost proudly I thought), then said, "So, what is it you think you're doing?"

"I don't know," I said. "She liked the car, you know."

"Don't play with me, Redding." Now, finally, he sat down and his face seemed to sag and he looked wearier than I'd ever seen him. "You're a good worker. You seem smart enough. I told you before it was about not fucking up. Remember?"

"Yes."

"Then why are you trying to so hard? First you assault my wife—her back still hurts her, you know." I didn't know. I hadn't seen her in the month since I found the camera. She'd never come back to work. "And now you take my daughter out in some death trap."

A distant ringing sounded far inside my head. I wanted to leap up and scream at him—who's the sicko here, Doc? Who put all this into play? But I could not make my mouth form the words, could not force the breath through my larynx.

He said, "You know what she told me? Our marriage was just, how did she put it—'an arrangement of housekeeping and a part-nership of business.'" His voice had risen to the point it bordered on the shrill, and he stared at me, not in anger anymore I thought but a kind of need—I had the clear sense that more than anything he just needed to talk about all this shit in his life and there was really no one else but me to listen. I mean, who else knew? He took some breaths then and calmed himself and said, "Let's not make it any harder on each other. All right?"

Outside the sun was well up and the heat of the air surprised me. In the parking garage I passed the special doctors' section at the front of the ground floor, Benzes and Porsches and Caddys. Especially nice was the big new silvery-green Beamer with the Path 1 license plate. I looked around. The shifts had already changed so I was alone. I stepped over to it, Ted's new car, gripped the antenna and pushed it forward until it snapped off.

* * *

She was not fat and doughy like her pretzels but thin to an unpleasant degree and pinched around the mouth and with streaked white and black hair that she tied back in the same manner my mother had. Perhaps it was a thing of working women, to have the hair neutralized in this way (Joyce's was a little too short to tie back and anyway she'd had the benefit of surgical caps when she needed). This woman had large coffee-stained teeth behind the pinched lips and wore a black polyester smock. She happened to be alone at this hour of the afternoon, before her student-girl employees came in to handle the rush of evening traffic. She simply looked at me, as if she sensed that I was not there to buy anything.

"My sister's name is Chloe Reed. She applied for a job here. Around the new year."

She shrugged and shook her head.

"She has a hemangioma on her face. A port-wine birthmark." I put my hand, fingers spread, over the right side of my face, spanning it from chin to eye, and her mouth opened and her eyes lit up with comprehension.

"I told her—"

"I know what you told her. You should be ashamed."

"Pardon me, young man—"

"I will *not* pardon you. Listen—saying that to a girl who obviously has struggled with this thing her whole life, who would be considered beautiful without it—who could do that?"

"I have a business to run."

"And I'm a law student." I waited a moment, let it sink in (for both of us; I had not premeditated this, had not in fact thought of it before that moment; it just popped out). "I've been discussing the situation with one of my professors. He seems to think it's actionable. And believe me, he's one who would know."

"What does that mean?"

"It means we can sue you for discrimination. You want to run your business, go ahead and run it—while you still can."

"Look—"

"*You* look," I said. "I understand that you have to sell pretzels to make a living. But who's to say that Chloe's working here is going to hurt sales? How do you know that?"

"People don't want to see—"

"You don't *know*. You don't know that at all. Try her one night a week."

"I—"

"One night a week. If sales fall, then let her go, no more questions asked. I won't show up here again. But just see."

I didn't work that night, and though I was up late I woke when it was still dark. In my dream there had been a loud noise, a sound like a fist, say, pounding on a door as someone walked past it. As I lay there, listening, the TV came on downstairs, too loudly for that early hour. I found Brigman in the living room tying his boots. He had on an old pair of Carhartt coveralls. For his new job, at a Gulf station owned by an Old Motorhead acquaintance of his named Freddy Garvey, he had to wear a navy shirt with his name in script on a patch on the left breast, and matching trousers.

He turned down the TV and said, "Freddy said he'll let me work on it, but you gotta help me get it over there."

So he'd waked me up as penance for my damaging the 'Cuda. When I broke it to him after he got home from work the night it happened he said nothing, though later he went down in the basement and pounded the shit out of something for a while.

"Help you?"

"Tow it. Ain't safe to drive. Have to use Sandy's car. I doubt yours has enough juice to pull anything besides itself."

I said, "Why so early?" He didn't have to be in until nine, so I didn't see why we couldn't have just taken it over then, and saved Chloe dropping him off on her way to school, which was how he'd been getting there.

"We're not exactly gonna be legal, or safe. I don't need us to get caught up in rush hour."

"All right."

"Get dressed."

The sky was open and clear and you could still see the stars, and though it was spring now the air this early still held a chill. I wore a thermal hooded sweatshirt under my denim jacket. We hooked the 'Cuda to the Skylark with twenty feet of chain and he sat behind the wheel so he could steer it and brake when I braked. I wondered if we got stopped would it be considered a violation— was steering a car that was being towed really driving?

In any case, we didn't get stopped. The station was dark. We left the 'Cuda, and on the way home he motioned for me to turn onto Dale Avenue, near our house, and then into the Red Dog Diner. We took a booth by the long window looking out on the parking lot. Brigman took out his pack of Marlboros with a book of matches tucked into the cellophane and laid it on the table. The waitress wore a brown nylon dress and white tights with a long run above one ankle. She brought Brigman a heavy bone-colored mug of coffee without asking and one for me, too, when I nodded. It had a dime-sized chip out of the rim that was stained the color of tobacco.

"Oatmeal," I told her.

"That it?" She looked at Brigman and said, "Usual?" He raised his chin.

I put my hands around the mug. Brigman shook a Marlboro from the pack and took up the matches and lit it and blew the first lungful out hard through his nose so that it struck the tabletop and spread out across it like a fog. A police cruiser raced silently past with its lights washing off the window glass of the cars in the lot. I took one of the Marlboros and lit it and said, "You ever thought of killing someone?"

"I did kill someone."

"I didn't mean like that. I didn't mean—"

"It don't matter. Don't got to pretend it didn't happen."

"I know. I meant something else."

In 1971 he bought a repossessed '70 Chevelle LS6 454 Big Block, one of the very hottest production cars ever manufactured in Detroit. After his modifications he figured it was putting out a fantastic 475 horsepower and 550 foot-pounds of torque. It hardly belonged on the street anymore, candy apple red with twin white stripes down its center (Donny, who would've been around sixteen, helped him paint it), a scoop, 1.65 Rockers, low-hanging glass packs Rally IIs. Even I could see that it was a kind of artwork, though one that would go from zero to sixty in well under four seconds and top out somewhere in that sparsely populated land north of one-eighty.

One night at Motorhead Brigman had some beers. He was not a drunk back then; though he drank, he was generally careful not to do it if he was racing. But on this night, after he'd started, a guy showed up from clear over in Muncie, Indiana, in a Goat loaded for bear. Brigman couldn't say no to it. Instead of going out somewhere in the country they torqued right down Reynolds Road, a four-lane west side strip that was busy even then. Coming up out of a railroad viaduct they happened onto a Valiant stalled in the right lane. Brigman's lane. There was an old couple sitting in it, waiting for a tow. The paper said they'd been married fifty-two years. The cops calculated that Brigman went into it still at around eighty. There wasn't much left of either car, nor of the old people. Brigman himself didn't regain consciousness for forty-eight hours but when he did he was all there but the spleen they'd had to remove to stop the bleeding, with two broken arms and some ribs. The city had been chasing Motorhead, so Brigman became a showcase for the prosecutors, a political stunt. His lawyer said normally on a first offense, even such an egregious one, you got probation, maybe loss of license. Brigman did six months with the county, and it was Sandy's life insurance that finally paid off the fine. The GTO from Muncie just kept going, and was not seen again in our city.

The waitress brought my meager bowl and a large oblong plat-
ter of eggs and bacon and hash browns with a side of buttered
toast for Brigman. We ate, me taking up small spoonfuls of the
oatmeal and blowing on them while Brigman bent over and shov-
eled hard and steady until his was mostly gone. Then he sat back
and pushed the plate away. He drank half the coffee, lit another
smoke, and said, "You can't think about that shit."

"What?"

"What you were talking about before. I know what you meant.
Just get all worked up when you know you ain't gonna do it because it ain't in you to." He tapped ashes onto his plate, where
they stuck to the remnants of the egg. "Maybe you could without
meaning it, you know, hit a guy so he falls and cracks his head or
something. But to think about it and then go do it, there's something missing in someone who can do that." He drank again from
the big mug. "You'd get caught anyway."

"Why?"

"I knew a guy when I was in, waitin' for his trial—cold ass
fucker and even he didn't get away with it."

"Some do."

Brigman nodded.

"I just meant did you ever want to?"

"Shit," he said, and laughed a bitter laugh and looked out the window at the new dawn. "Best to just let it go, you know? Let it pass."

I was pulled upward out of a long deep library night before my
last two exams by the sensation of someone hovering behind me,
and turned to find Jessi there.

"I'm really sorry," she said. "I know you're busy and I'm bug-
ging you, but I just saw you here and . . . I wanted to thank you
for the other day, and apologize."

It was Thursday, three days since our near wreck, and though I'd
meant to call her on every one of those days, though I had taken her
father's ignorance as some small hope that I still had a chance to use

her, I had not called and suspected it was due to some last shred of decency or perhaps the instinct of self-preservation, some final urge not to destroy the life I was trying to build for myself.

"Apologize?" I said. "I'm the one . . ."

She shook her head and looked contrite, as if she were waiting for me to send her away or bludgeon her with my tongue—to humiliate her again. And I understood what her presence meant. She hadn't just stumbled across me. I'd told her enough about my life—she knew where I hid. I'd endangered her and made her sick but it was she who felt she'd failed, felt shamed, felt she needed to make amends. But of course she would, I thought. Who was she, after all? And I saw then that I'd read it all wrong, read her all wrong, and yet my ennui or whatever it was had led me to play it just right.

"It's okay," I said, "but don't come here like this again."

She stared at her feet.

"Do you understand?"

"Yes." A whisper.

"Come on," I said and stood up.

"Are you sure?"

"Didn't I ask?"

"Yes." Whispered again.

I'd been there already six hours. It would be enough or it wouldn't, and what difference would it make anyway now? All the As in the world weren't going to help me after this. It was one of those rare clear junctions, a point from which I could see the consequences of either choice, to be smart and safe and to go forward toward what I'd been working for, or to shoot my wad on a righteous but unwinnable fight.

I took her to the union, where they sold low beer and never carded. Even low worked eventually. She wobbled when we got up. Outside, I slipped my hand beneath her puffy arm and squeezed.

At her car, I said, "You sure you can drive?"

"Yes."

"I'll follow you anyway."

"That's so sweet."

She pressed herself to me and turned her face up. Though it had a certain hunger behind it, hers was not the aggressive expert mouth of her mother. She opened it too wide, for one thing, so that the suction wasn't right, and then just held it against mine in all its softness and flaccidity, a wet hole waiting for me to fill it. When I did not, her tongue fluttered across my teeth, probed tentatively beyond them, but I kept mine well back in its own dark cave, withheld. The beer bubbled in my belly.

She drove me to my car in a far lot and leaned across and kissed me once more. Then I followed her as promised and pulled into the driveway behind her, though I stopped out near the road. Through the trees the great house looked as impressive as in the daylight, but different—warm lamplight streamed from the windows of both parlor and library and from the entrance and two upstairs rooms. As I watched, the light from an upper window dimmed as if someone had passed before it or perhaps stopped to look out. Jessi pulled back to the garage. I sat for another moment or two watching and thought to myself that I had done exactly what I'd set out to do. It was set up now. It was set. What remained was only to let it unfold. The beer turned again and now it was I who had to open the door and lean out. It came up then, propelled by vicious contractions, and splashed stinking and hot there on the asphalt at the end of the doctor's driveway.

TEN

A black woman in a white uniform, her face shiny with sweat, looked up from a stove heaped with pans and skillets.

"Hiya, Rose," Jessi said. "This is Syd. Everything all right?"

"Everything fine," Rose said and huffed and bent back to her cooking.

In a breezeway beyond the kitchen Jessi plucked at my shirt and said, "She's just the cleaning lady but they like to show off for these brunches every Saturday—'oh, look, we even have our own cook.' "

Through a window and then a sliding glass door the breezeway looked over a sun porch that held a suite of rattan furniture, a table for ten, and several chaise longues and armchairs. Ted held down the head of the table. Around him sat several comfortable-looking middle-aged couples. Beyond the porch, past the garage, a pool shimmered in the morning sunlight. I didn't see Joyce.

"Doctors," Jessi said, in answer to my unasked question.

"Hey, that's Masterson," I said.

"You know him?"

"He's my adviser. I thought he was a Ph.D."

"He is. He taught anatomy at Case when my dad went there."

"Are you kidding?"

"No. That's his wife, Dotty. I don't know any of the others."

"What about me?"

"I know you. You're not a doctor yet."

"Really? I meant, have you said anything?"

"I said I was bringing someone I'd seen a couple of times but it was a surprise."

I followed her out, and though I felt Ted watching me he did not move or utter any sound.

"Jessi," Masterson said, and stood and hugged her and congratulated her on her imminent graduation, then turned to me and shook my hand and said, "Already dating the boss's daughter."

To his wife, I said, "Dr. Masterson's my adviser at the U."

Dotty beamed. I looked at Ted. He wore khakis and an Izod shirt and over them a navy silk dressing gown. He glared, eyes extruded, face burning, but was cool enough to just sit there and choke out the other introductions.

Dotty said, "We've already started. Go on and eat, you two."

The table held a large cut-glass bowl of bagels and smaller matching bowls of flavored cream cheeses, platters of lox and bacon and sausages and freshly pressed waffles, a chafing dish of scrambled eggs, bowls of grated cheeses and chives and sour cream and capers and onions, pitchers of hand-squeezed orange and grapefruit juice and a decanter of coffee. It was kind of sick, really. I'd worked buffets like this at the club but never imagined seeing one in someone's house. I took only coffee and sat next to Jessi on a chaise. I was looking out at the pool when someone came out and one of the other women said, "Joyce."

"I'm sorry," she said, "I was just . . ."

She held a hand beside her face but not quite touching it, as if she had reached there for something and then forgot in mid-gesture what it was.

"So have you met the new boyfriend?" Masterson said.

"Oh, they know each other," said Jessi, "from when Mom was working. Syd even rescued us once. We were broken down and he saw us and fixed the car right there on the road."

That old look of long-pain-endured, the one I loved, came into

Joyce's face. I found I had missed it, and that I was glad to be able to watch her again. I had always been glad to watch her, even from before the time we first spoke over the body of a hundred-year-old woman, from the first time I saw her before I had any idea who she was.

She said, "Well, hello, Syd," and then looked at her husband (who clearly had not informed her of his discovery that I'd been driving their daughter). She stepped forward and I thought then that she would fall. Several of the men leapt to catch her but she did not fall, though her face had gone chalky. They helped her into a chair and one of them poured her a glass of juice.

"I'm fine," she said, waving it away. "I don't know what's wrong with me."

"She hasn't been well," said Ted. "That back injury. You should rest."

She nodded but looked at me. I thought the incredible crackling in the air must be audible but none of the others seemed to notice anything. She said, "I am so terribly sorry. But I believe I am going to go lie down," and stood up to leave.

"Let me help you," Ted said, but Joyce did not wait for him. As he followed her out he threw me a long last gaze, more of curiosity and surprise, I thought, or regard even, than of anger or angst.

Not much later (though long enough for me, appetite recovered, to dive into that feast) Jessi and I excused ourselves. As we passed the staircase in the foyer I heard, far up inside the great house somewhere, the faintest sound of shouting or screaming and a concurrent tinkling that sounded very much like something, a small ornate mirror, say, or a cut-glass decanter, smashing as if it had been thrown against a wall.

I dressed early for work and watched TV with Brigman. That afternoon I'd found him smoking again at the front door. He said, "That woman called."

"What woman?"

"About them pretzels."

I wanted to shout but in respect of his paternal frown and the badness he was so afraid would come at Chloe in the world, I just slipped upstairs and found her in her room. She squealed and threw her arms around me—she kept saying she couldn't believe that after all this time the woman would just call like that out of the blue. She was only getting one four-hour shift a week to start, but she didn't seem to care.

Now, as Brigman and I watched and he smoked (somehow managing to fret and sit still at the same time), the phone rang.

"Oh, my god," Jessi said. "They are so weird."

"What happened?" After brunch we went to the old Stranahan Estate, which was now owned by the city, and walked trails, and as we walked she let her hand brush against mine until I took it.

"They were waiting when I came home. My dad started in about older men and what business did I have and I was leaving soon anyway for Cleveland and mixing business with pleasure. I guess because you work for him he thinks it's inappropriate for us to go out. I said that was stupid and he got really pissed but I don't get it. Since when do they care, anyway? But the weirdest thing was my mom. She just sat there until I said I really liked you, and she started crying." She waited, then said, "Syd?"

"I'm here."

"It won't scare you off from seeing me? I mean, if you want to. Keep on, I mean. Seeing me."

"I do. Want to."

"Really?"

"Yeah."

I was crossing the top open floor of the parking garage to the stairs when a car squealed hard off the ramp and stopped in front of me. The door opened and I felt the old fight or flight, then recognized the car.

"I don't know what you think you're doing," Ted said, his damaged arm resting on the roof, "but it's going to stop."

I said, "Are you threatening me?"

"You certainly aren't doing yourself any good."

"I guess that's my problem."

"You will not see her again."

"Isn't that up to her?"

"It's up to me. She'll do what I tell her to do."

"I guess I heard something different."

"Don't fuck with me, Syd. You have no idea."

"I had no idea, Dr. Kessler," I said. "Ted. But I do now."

"Who do you think you are?"

"Nobody. We both know that. The question is, who are you to think you can do whatever you want to people and no one will say anything?"

"You have proof of nothing."

"What I have is your daughter."

He sneered then or grimaced; in any case it was a hideous face that I found I liked on him. A security car pulled up beside us. The guard said, "Everything okay? Oh, hi, Dr. Kessler."

"We're fine," he said. "I had to drop in for something and ran into Mr. Redding here. He just needed some advice."

"All right," she said, and went past us and turned around and came back slowly so she could look at me. Ted said, "You'll get hurt. I told you the other morning, and I came by to tell you again, to give fair warning, but this is it. Stop it, now."

I walked backward toward the stairwell, facing him, and said, "There's something I wonder if you've thought about in this, Doc. In the end, of the two of us, who really has more to lose?"

The following Friday I grilled cheese sandwiches and heated tomato soup for Chloe's and my supper and put the rest of the soup in a Thermos and a couple of the sandwiches in Brigman's old black steel lunch box and had Chloe drive us to Garvey's Gulf. Brigman seemed happy to see us—he was in a good mood, anyway. We sat together at the greasy cluttered glass counter while he ate and Chloe and I drank cold Cokes from the slot-pull bottle machine. Things seemed to have changed since she got the job (which was a success apparently—she'd already been moved up to twelve hours a week, including one weekend shift). I hadn't seen her with Donny at all, and she acted as if she actually wanted us for her family again. I had the wild hope that now with her being engaged in the world more, her relationship with boys in general could take a rest. So we were all there together, even the cars, Sandy's Skylark in the lot and the 'Cuda in the bay beside us. (I'd cracked a rocker arm, it turned out, or rather it had cracked under me. It'd been going to go anyway, Brigman said, and he was doing a whole suspension and alignment job on it in his spare time.) Freddy came out of his office then to say hey and ask how things were going. He was always around on Fridays to bag the register proceeds every hour and throw them in the safe. Freddy was okay, though, and in addition to letting Brigman work on the 'Cuda he didn't say much if Brigman came in late or took a little extra break—it turned out Brigman was bringing in some business, guys who remembered him from the old days and liked the idea of someone like that working on their station wagons—so it looked like Brigman might stay employed this time for a while.

It was all too happy. We were like some goddamn gas station Brady Bunch sitting there together around the dingy dinner table.

"Doing any surgeries yet?" Freddy asked me.

"Not authorized ones."

"You get as good on bodies as your old man here is on cars, you won't be able to spend it all."

"We'll help him," Chloe said.

I said, "Hand me the board." It was a grimy eight-inch length of two by four with a hole drilled in one end and the rest room key chained to it, I guess so no one walked off with it. The bathrooms were around at the rear, alongside a pile of worn tires and a couple of rusted engine blocks and the decaying carcass of an old Mustang.

I had a date. Jessi and I had met for lunch earlier in the week, clandestinely but not far from her house, at a Coney Island restaurant. She suggested we meet somewhere Friday away from the house to avoid aggravating her parents, but I sulked, squeezed out all the hurt inside me for her to see, and after a few minutes of my silence she asked what was wrong. I asked if it was wrong of me to want to ring her bell like any other guy, to have a normal date instead of some sneaky tryst. I said, "If we set the pattern now, it'll always be that way." It was terribly effective, demonstrating not only strength on my part but a whiff of the suggestion of commitment, of looking forward to more us.

"You're right," she said, finally. Her voice was hushed and throaty, and she would not look at me. "Come get me. Please."

The concrete floor of the men's room was damp, the air perfused with the stench of piss. Fingers of rust pointed down from the top of the urinal. I breathed through my mouth. On the condom machine a bounteously racked lingerie-clad woman threw back her head and laughed as she embraced her man—she knew what was coming. Safety! Strength! Sensitivity! the sign shouted, and all for a quarter. I looked at it for a moment, then dug out the change I made sure was in my pocket before coming over here so I didn't have to embarrass myself asking for it.

No one answered. I pressed the button again and again before finally hearing feet pounding down the staircase. Jessi opened the door, her face red and her bangs hanging in her eyes.

"They are such assholes!" she whisper-hissed. "I'm sorry. I'm not quite ready, as if you couldn't tell."

"It's okay." I went in and when she ran back up the stairs I stepped further into the deadly quiet, and listened, and then stepped into the darkened library, which I'd never been in before. It was maybe the best room in the house, I decided, with high rows of oak shelving all around and the ladder and leather furniture and an antique library table and a huge roll-top desk that must have been worth some kind of fortune. I dragged my fingers down across the rows of rounded slats, then noticed a wooden bar on the far wall, with shelves of liquor behind it. I had just started over to examine them when Ted, from the doorway, said, "What are you doing?"

"Just looking at all your nifty stuff."

"You have no business."

"No business looking? That's a good one, Dr. Kessler."

It threw him, that line. Though he was backlighted I knew it from the pause and then the tightness in his voice—"I want you out of here"—at the edges of which I heard the first fraying of his control.

I said, "She'll be ready in a minute, then we'll go."

"Do you really think you're going to get away with this?"

"With what?"

"Whatever it is you think you're doing."

"But what is that? What is it *you* think I'm doing?" As I walked toward him he backed up a step or two into the foyer, so now I could see his expressions tightening and twisting in on themselves. I said, "Maybe I'm sincere."

Ted aimed a finger and said, "I can fuck you up."

"Have someone smash up my expensive car? Embarrass me in front of all my esteemed colleagues? Molest my daughter?"

"Get out."

I thought of what Brigman had said, how Ted had learned to kill with his hands, but I was surprised to feel nothing, no sweating, no quaking, no thudding heart. I'd never before felt the coldness that ran through me (though I have since then). I simply waited. But Ted didn't move. I stood still, taking in that moment of the cracking of his facade, then went toward him again. When I was close enough to see the veins in his nose, I said, "I don't know when she'll be home, Ted. You never know what might come up."

His hook jerked up toward me but stopped between us. We

both looked down at it. I said, "I heard you cut your own arm off. Is that true?"

"She's not going with you."

"I think she is. You just don't know where. But, oh, if you did."

He opened his mouth but the stairs creaked and Joyce said, "That's enough." She came over and touched his arm and he turned and walked off a few steps toward the dining room.

"Two, three in the morning, I figure," I said, "by the time we're done."

He spun back but Joyce said to him, "Go!" and then to me, "You stop it! Now! Both of you stop it!"

"Stop what, Joyce?" I said. "Do you even know?"

Ted remained in the dining room doorway.

"Hey," I said, "I know. How about if I make you guys a video-tape? That'll give you a good idea. You might even learn something from it."

She started to cry then. I knew she would. I'd worn a light jacket against the evening chill and reached into the pocket now for my handkerchief and pulled it out to offer it to her, and as I did the condom I'd folded inside it fell onto the wooden floor between us. We looked at it, the three of us, lying there in all its red-wrapped tawdriness.

"Oopsy," I said. Then I heard Jessi. I scooped it up as she came down, her eyes wide.

"I don't get you," she said to them and that had to be the simple truth. How could she have fathomed such anger and resistance to this simple thing of our dating?

"Please don't go," Joyce said.

"*Why?*" she said, and now she was close to tears, too. "Why are you doing this to me? What is *wrong* with you?"

"Just . . . trust us," Joyce said.

"Why can't you trust me?"

Ted said, "Enough. You don't talk to your mother like that. You're not going. That's all there is to it."

"I am going," she said.

Joyce said, "Then you don't need to come back here."

"Oh, *stop* it!" Ted said to her. "Just shut up, will you?"

Jessi regarded them, then turned to me and said, "Can we go?" and she went, leaving me to follow. I lingered a moment, looked at them, then said, "Don't wait up."

For greatest effect I needed to keep her out late and wasn't sure at first how to engineer it—she couldn't get into bars or clubs for a couple more weeks, when she turned eighteen. With a slow dinner and a late movie I could stretch it to midnight, and had resigned myself to that when I heard some X-ray techs at work laughing about *The Rocky Horror Picture Show*. It ran at midnight every Friday down in the old Anselm Theater, which had become (appropriately) a porn house except when it sold out showing camp to fans who recited dialogue and screamed at the actors, brought squirt guns and toast and newspapers to act out scenes and dressed in drag. Jessi squealed when I suggested it. First we had pizza and walked around the mall. From some distance I made out Chloe in her brown smock, her hair in a white gauze net, behind the counter of The Pretzel Man. She was busy, so I didn't go over. I didn't want her to see me with Jessi anyway. When the mall closed, I bought an eight of Shoenlings and we took it to the Ottawa Park golf course, not far from the theater, and parked and walked in and drank sitting on a bench at the first tee. She put her face against my arm, her breath dampening my sleeve, then turned and said, "Well, now you've got me tipsy in a deserted park."

"Are you scared?"

"No."

"I am."

She laughed, and I laughed at her laughing. She said, "Are you going to take advantage of me?"

"Should I?"

"That's a complicated question. And there's the other one."

"What's that?"

"Do you want to?"

She kissed me then. I kissed her back some but when she moved her hand across my chest I pulled away.

"You're strange," she said.

"You noticed."

"I mean, most guys just look for an opening. But you have respect, and self-control. You're amazing. You're going to make a great doctor."

"That's me," I said. "Just full of respect."

We kissed again a little bit, and then it was late and time thankfully to go.

I didn't get her home until nearly two-thirty. I needed us to sit there for enough time that something could seem to happen (I had no doubt Ted was up) but she was understandably nervous. I said, "I want to do something for your birthday and graduation and all."

"You don't have to. Really."

"I was thinking—" What I was thinking was how badly I wanted to avoid some emotional thing. And I'd had an idea. "—I heard the Ramones are going to be here . . ." So much for emotion, I figured. But she screamed and grabbed me.

"Oh, my god!" she said. "Oh, my god! Can you get tickets? I heard it was sold out already."

I pulled them out, two scalped seats for Friday, June 30, at a place called Debbie's Domino Club. So of course it required us making out again and this time it went on some, until finally I pulled her over the parking brake onto my lap so that she was straddling me—and though of course we were fully clothed I thought that perhaps in the dark through binoculars from an upstairs window that detail might be open to interpretation. Finally she said she had to go in. I walked her to the door. She touched my face. We said nothing.

In my car, I reached under the seat for the baggie I'd stashed there. Inside it was another of the condoms I'd bought at Garvey's. I had used it, filled it in my bedroom before I came over here (filled it imagining Joyce) and sealed the open end with a paper clip, which I now removed. I opened my window and tossed the slimy thing up on the walkway where it would be clearly visible to whoever came out first in the morning to get the Saturday paper, and who I was pretty sure wouldn't be Jessi.

ELEVEN

It was not my plan to precipitate some crisis or blowup but rather to let it linger, to keep it lodged in their craws, them wondering if I was out doing to her the worst things they could imagine. So in the next week I saw her only once. We met for dinner, since for some reason I was not invited to the big family graduation/birthday gig they threw. After that dust settled, we took to meeting every second or third afternoon.

I had been considering my next thrust when on the day before her birthday she let me pick her up at home. We drove far out of town to a huge disorganized used-book store and spent the afternoon browsing. It was nice, actually. It was brilliant out that evening when we returned, clear and sunny and vibrant. In the driveway, as she leaned back against the Datsun, waiting for my usual insipid peck on the lips, I noticed a face again in one of the upstairs windows, and a dual refraction that was just maybe the long late sunlight coming off binocular lenses. I grabbed Jessi and mashed my mouth to hers. It had been pretty chaste between us since that necking in my car the night of *Rocky Horror.* I made it deep and long and even ground into her a little.

When I let up, she said, "Well, hello, Mr. Syd."

I just looked at her. She smiled as if she knew something, as if something new had come to light.

The next night Kathy was on again, so Ray and I pretty much had the lounge to ourselves. Sometime after one when things had slowed and we were having coffee I said, "You hear about when Kessler came in a couple weeks ago on a Saturday night?"

"No. What the hell for?"

"To talk to me. He cornered me in the parking garage."

"What?" Ray was reading an old *Sports Illustrated* with his feet up on the table, but he put them down.

"I've been going out with his daughter. Did you know that?"

"How would I know that?"

"I don't know. Shit gets around."

"Well, not that shit. That's why he cornered you, for taking her out? He ought to be kissing your ass."

"Well, he's not. I might get fired."

Ray slapped the table and said, "You know, there's an office here called labor management. They'd love to hear about this."

"No," I said, "it's probably better."

"Syd—are you guys serious?"

"I guess."

"I've met her a couple times. She doesn't seem like your type, if you want to know the truth. Sort of prissy rich, you know. I mean, no offense."

"No. I know what you mean."

Then he sat back and grinned. He was a reliable guy, Ray, and he didn't disappoint me. "You getting some off her?"

I shrugged.

"Is that what it's about?"

I nodded.

"What, you can't get any ass but Kessler's daughter?"

"Sure," I said. "But—" I shook my head. "You never had any like this."

"Don't bet on it."

"Then maybe you have. So you know."

"What?"

I leaned in and lowered my voice and said, "Ray, she's crazy."

"She likes it?"

"I mean she can't get enough. She's a nympho. My dick's about to fall off."

He whooped and slapped the table again.

I said, "I need a vacation from it."

"So, details. Let's hear it."

I shook my head.

"Oh, come on. What are you, a gentleman now?"

"Anything," I said.

"What?"

"That's what she lets me do."

"Bullshit."

"You name it."

"No."

"I mean it. Name something, anything you can think of. If I wanted, she'd do it. Probably already have."

Ray looked at me strangely and shook his head.

I said, "I've even asked her things, you know, just to see how far I could push it."

Ray stood up and put his hands on his head and was pacing the length of the room when Kathy came in. To me, she said, "What's got him going?"

"Jesus," Ray said, "you don't want to know."

"Probably not."

"About Syd the Stud."

"Oh, goodie, boy talk," she said as she filled her mug. "Syd has a girlfriend and Ray the Masher gets to hear about it."

"He's going out with Kessler's daughter."

She looked at me and said, "Jessi?"

"Yeah, baby," said Ray.

"You're not doing anything with her."

"Right," Ray said.

"Are you?"

I shrugged.

"I told you," Ray said, and laughed in her face.

"God," Kathy said, "she's still in high school."

"She just graduated."

"Still," said Kathy, "you could have a little respect."

"Oh, fuck that," Ray said. "How old is she?"

"Eighteen, today actually."

"So what's wrong with it?"

"I just think that's a little young to be taking advantage."

"It doesn't sound like he's the one taking advantage," Ray said, and laughed again.

"What's going on?" Kathy said. "What are you two doing?"

"About everything, it sounds like," said Ray.

She sat down at the table and looked at me seriously. "What is it, Syd?"

"Nothing," I said, "that she doesn't want."

"Jessi Kessler?"

"She's kind of wild, Kathy."

"You're lying."

"I'm not," I said. "I like her, you know. She's a nice person. It was just kind of an accident that we started going out at all. But then it's just become, I don't know—"

"Slam-o-*rama!*" Ray said.

"Shut *up,* Ray," Kathy said. "Everything's such a goddamn joke with you. I think this is serious."

"Yeah, it sounds serious to me," he said.

She grunted in frustration and pushed herself up, stalked to the door, then turned and said, "Listen, Syd, I don't know what's really going on. I always thought you were a nice guy. And what you do in your private life is your business. But it's only your business, you know? Sitting here telling this jerk about it is kind of scummy. I thought you were better than that." She left.

Ray looked at me a moment, then said, "Yeah, you fucking lowlife. What's wrong with you? So, okay, now I want details."

I gave him some.

Later, near dawn, I came down to find Ray in the blood bank. Kathy was sitting at the bench and he was leaning over her, his lips near her ear. It was historic. After I clocked out I heard the cacophony of snitches buzzing in the lounge. I went down to listen but it wasn't necessary. I knew what all the fuss was about.

I'd've killed to see the look on his face, and I wanted to know, though of course I couldn't exactly, how the rumors came to him. It had to've been through Barb—"Um, Dr. Kessler, you know, people are talking . . . there's this rumor, uh, about your daughter? I just thought you should know." How would he have looked at that moment? What would he have said and, more intriguing, what would he have revealed about how it wounded him (and there was no doubt, there never has been, that it wounded him)? For though he relied on Barb's nosiness and nastiness and her pleasure at serving his compulsions and whims, I do not think he particularly admired her or trusted her or wanted anything from her other than that she venerate him and grovel and snitch and maybe give him a little sugar now and then (though when I discovered the truth about Ted and Joyce's games I have to say it cast some doubt on the Ted-Barb tryst theory). Anyway, I suspect that the thought of revealing anything too personal to her, or anyone in that lab, would have horrified him. But now (presumably) here it was, laid out by her right on his desk. "Everyone's talking about it—what she's doing with Syd Redding—that *he's* doing . . . things to her. Awful things. That she *lets* him." (This is, of course, conjecture on my part, but over the many years since then I've learned things, gathered bits here and there.) Would she have been graphic? One of the myriad of small ironies was that as the co-subject of these rumors I was not directly privy to them, though

Ray fed me pieces that floated back to him. I knew what I'd told him, of course (and it wasn't really all that much, composed as much of innuendo as actual images, though I'll grant that some of those images were on the odd side), but we know what happens to rumors when they propagate. On that I had counted.

My disappointment was that, aside from not knowing the details of how Ted found out, I couldn't even see how he looked because he was gone. The day after the rumors broke, he stopped coming to the lab. This was in itself remarkable—he only ever stayed away when he was out of town, and I knew he wasn't out of town. I mentioned it one night that week to Phyllis, that I hadn't seen him around. (I didn't suppose she'd heard the rumors. She wasn't the sort anyone would have cared to tell.)

"I don't know what's wrong with him," she said. "He must be sick but I haven't heard. Not like him." Sick, I thought. Sickened would have been more accurate. As I had been. Ted, I hoped, I dreamed, was feeling something approaching the rage/shame/blind-anger/bitterness I'd been dealt.

At first it merely thrilled me, but as his absence stretched to a week I became almost frightened at how deeply I must have wounded him, that I had cut him in probably the most devastating manner I could have conceived. It surely affected him more this way than if I'd actually but quietly done the things to Jessi I claimed. I'd made Ted and his family a kind of prurient spectacle in front of his subjects. It was perfect, really.

I wanted to catch at least a glimpse of him but Jessi insisted now that we meet away from the mansion, leading me to gather that things were not pleasant and getting less so. It had begun to become familiar between us and all she said she wanted to do that Saturday night was take some beer to Ottawa Park where we'd drunk before. I talked her into seeing a movie first (*Grease*), then bought an eight and we went.

It was a city golf course but also a park, part of it, with a broad triangular-shaped section of playground equipment and sand boxes and horseshoe pits set off from the grounds of the course by a small angling road on one side and a creek on another. It was on this road that we parked, a dark spot known for car trysts and so patrolled fairly regularly by the city cops.

We drank a couple of the Schoenlings in the car, then went tripping into the night. She wanted to play on the canvas swings first (she swung with her feet out and her head tipped back so that her hair brushed the ground), then made me go back to my car and get the blanket in my trunk because the thought of sitting on the bare ground was icky. We crossed the creek on an arched wooden bridge and wound farther into the darkness and hills until settling on the leeward slope of a ridge exposed to the half-moon so that it wasn't especially dark. I was afraid I knew what was coming, but just lay back and sipped a beer and watched the sky. We did not talk much and that part of it was pleasant, but then, of course, she leaned over and started to kiss me and soon she was playing with my shirt and then I felt her fingers graze my belt buckle. They did not do anything there, just touched it by way of suggesting, I suppose, that things were allowed to move in that direction. I did not touch her. She pulled away and took off her glasses and then she did a surprising thing—she sat up and unbuttoned her blouse (I could see her clearly) and took it off, then reached behind herself to undo her bra.

"What are you doing?" I said.

"Undressing. Is that all right?"

"I—" I froze. I said, "What was that?"

She was quiet, having heard it, too—what sounded to me exactly like the sliding of a shoe on slightly damp golf course grass in the middling moonlight.

But she said, "Nothing."

"It was."

"Are you scared?"

"No, of course not."

She took her bra off then. She had nice breasts, I'll say that, the breasts of a slightly overweight just-turned-eighteen-year-old, which is to say that they were more substantial than the typical breasts of a young woman of average weight and yet still retained all the firmness and height and profile of the newly budded, with nipples (pale they appeared in that light) that tipped ever so slightly moonward and underbulges that hung ever so nicely earthward and round lateral edges that extended beyond her chest wall so that if she were to turn away from you and raise her arms slightly you would still be able to see the arcs of them protruding from the sides. This was, to a twenty-three-year old man whose lover had betrayed him terribly so that for weeks and weeks on end he'd had nothing but the dry appeasement of his own rosy palm, one mighty enticing sight. Then she stood and unzipped her jeans.

"Jessi!" I said.

"Syd, I'm ready. I want this. I want you."

"And I want you."

"Okay, then," and the jeans slid down to reveal silken pale panties (well, I imagined them as silken, though in that ancient light it was impossible to say for sure—they had that shine of silk, though I suppose, of course, they could have been rayon or something) and her ever-so-slightly pouty but still firm little belly and the ridges of what appeared to be quite a womanly set of hips. Oh, my own jeans felt small.

I said, "Jessi—it's not . . . it's not time for this yet."

"Yes, it is."

"Don't you think it's something we should discuss?"

"We need to discuss this?"

"Yes."

"Syd, are you a virgin?"

"God. No."

"Well, neither am I. So what's the problem?"

"It's—I just don't want to do anything wrong. I don't want to hurt you."

"I don't think it'll hurt."

"Please—"

"It's my father, isn't it?"

"No—"

"He's got you scared."

"Jessi, stop it. It's not that at all. It's just, you."

"You don't want me."

"No. I mean, yes! It's not that."

"It is." She pulled the jeans back up and fastened them (bye-bye silken panties; bye-bye hips) and snatched up her bra and turned away to re-attach it (so long, beautiful breasts) and put on her blouse and stalked back toward the car as she buttoned it. I gathered what was left of the beers and chased her, calling out, but she began to run and by the time I got to the car she was already there and seat-belted in, arms crossed over her chest, staring mutely ahead into the darkness.

I didn't hear from her the next day (she generally called if I failed to call her). With Brigman at the garage much of the time either working for real or working on the 'Cuda, Chloe (who was putting in twenty hours a week now for the Pretzel Bitch) and I blew the hearts out of some perfectly functional weekdays watching TV and smoking cigarettes and sipping beers. On this very morning of Jessi not calling, Chloe said to me, out of nowhere and apropos of nothing, "Do you have a girlfriend?"

"Why?"

"Just, do you?"

"No."

"That's not what I heard. Someone saw you with a girl at the mall. You were holding hands."

"So?"

"So do you?"

"Holding hands doesn't mean anything."

"It means something."

"Something, but not necessarily they're your girlfriend."

"A da-ate."

"Whatever."

"Is that who calls here sometimes?"

"Yeah."

"Are you having sex with her?"

"Jesus, Chloe."

"That means you are."

"I'm not. And she's not my girlfriend."

"How old is she?"

"Old enough."

"I heard she's still in high school."

"Where do you hear this?"

"Is she?"

"No."

"When did she graduate?"

"Last week."

"And you talk about me and Donny?"

"You're sixteen."

"And what's she, seventeen?"

"Eighteen."

"As of?"

"Week before last."

"So she was seventeen when you started."

"Was it true what Brigman said about Donny?"

"No."

"But you were seeing him."

"Are."

"What?"

She looked at me with a pained expression and shook her head at my global cluelessness, and said, "Am. Is."

"Still?"

"Don't do anything stupid, all right?"

"He'll find out. He found out before."

"Only because Donny was trying to be decent about it."

"Donny told him?"

"And god what a mistake that was."

"You should wait anyway."

"Till when I'm seventeen in like two months?"

So she'd made her point—that it was no different really than what I was doing, and if I thought she should stop, then I should stop, too. And she was right, but for different reasons. I didn't know whether the pit in my stomach was from the images of my sister and Donny the Dumb or of a girl who was falling in some kind of love with a guy who'd led her under very false pretenses into thinking he cared something for her but had instead just set about giving her the reputation of a deviant nymphomaniac.

On Monday Ted showed up finally, bearing not the look I had been anticipating but one of haleness and vigor. "Syd," he said in the hallway. He practically opened his arms to me but allowed a pat on the shoulder to suffice. Phyllis looked suspicious when he pumped her hand as if they'd been missing each other for years. "It's good to be back," he said.

"Where were you?" she asked.

"Nowhere," he said. "I didn't go anywhere. Just stayed home, did some writing, reading, caught up on a lot. And man, I feel good. Mental health week, let's call it."

She nodded, regarding him.

"You should take one," he said. "Worlds of good." He looked at me again and winked before prancing off to Chemistry. A little later Ray wandered up and said, "What the fuck's up with him?"

I was afraid I knew, but wasn't sure until I was putting away my tray in the equipment room. The student part-timers and regular day-shifters were loading theirs when Ted came in and over to me. He straightened the lapels on my lab coat and said, "Walk you out?" It got very quiet.

In the hallway he walked close beside me and as we came to the door to the back stairwell, said, "I've always trusted her. The fact that you made me doubt that for the first time is a shame. But at least now I see how full of shit you really are."

He knew I hadn't laid a hand on her, that the only ones I'd been

fucking with were him and Joyce, and he'd called my bluff. I
didn't even have the presence of mind to try to bluff back, to fake
like he was wrong or even to act like I didn't care. I just nodded
blankly and wandered off.

I had classes all morning (it was the summer of Statistics, Physics,
and Genetics), so I didn't get to sleep until the afternoon, and
woke when it was getting dark. When I got to work, Ray caught
me in the stockroom and said Barb was going around saying I'd
made it all up.

"You listen to her?" I said.

"No. But are you? Seeing Jessi Kessler?"

"Yeah."

I knew he wanted to ask the next question, whether I'd been
bullshitting him about her or not, but it would've been an asshole
thing to ask and we both knew he wasn't going to. It was up to me
to volunteer something more, and by so doing ameliorate Barb's
anti-rumors, begin my counter-counter-offensive. When I didn't
say anything, Ray left.

In the morning, stares and whispers pinged around me. A bench
tech who with the first round of rumors had taken to calling me
Dr. Stud, now said, "Dr. Dud," and laughed. It was that kind of
juvenile shit. I felt sickened, not at what they said or even what
they thought (I mean, really), but at being shamed once more by
Ted. He had turned it around, reversed it so it was I now who had
become the prurient spectacle, the lab joke-butt of the week.

I felt like getting drunk and thought about asking Ray to go out
but then thought better of it because if we drank the subject
would surely come up and then I'd either have to tell him I used
him by lying to him, or else lie to him some more, and I really
didn't feel like doing either one.

Jessi left messages that I did not return, and the week passed
until that Friday, the day of the Ramones concert.

TWELVE

"I'm surprised," she said, when I called. "I wasn't sure you remembered."

"Why wouldn't I? You still want to go, don't you?"

"I don't know. I guess."

"Are we or not?" I snapped, and as it had in the library the annoyance in my voice did something to her.

"Yes," she said, softer.

"I should get you by eight."

She said she'd be waiting at the end of her driveway, so could I please not be late, then hung up. My teeth ached.

When I got there, though, she wasn't at the end of the driveway at all but inside somewhere so that I had to park and go up and knock and who should answer the door but Ted himself.

"Oh, ho," he said, "did you forget something?"

"Jessi, actually."

He did his best to carry on the act from the hospital but with no audience to play to he was pretty transparent, redness creeping up his neck, the muscles in his jaw working.

"Really?" he said. "Playing that game again?"

"I bought her tickets to a concert for her birthday. It's tonight."

"Well, have fun. And maybe afterward you'll have time for a walk in the park." Then he slapped my arm as if we were the best old buddies in the world.

Jessi came down the stairs. "Oh," she said, "I see you've met my father."

The tickets turned out to be a great deal, given that the opening act alone seemed to go on for hours. It was a local band that had discovered in punk the thesis that music was egalitarian, that you didn't even really have to know how to play an instrument to make a band. So they didn't. At the end of it (finally) the guitarist brilliantly smashed his guitar and the lead singer just as brilliantly threw the mike stand into the crowd. People cheered and held up their middle fingers. Debbi's Domino Club, a place I'd never heard of before, was a pole barn on a gravel lot on a dirt road far out east of the east side. Tables and chairs sat crammed onto broad risers around an open section in the front where people could dance or just stand and look at the band, and waitresses came by and took your money. Jessi and I sat and drank and did not talk (not that we could've heard anything anyway).

The second act, the Fabulous Poodles, was a gimmick band with a catchy single called "Rumbaba Boogie," but they were English, I think, and at least knew how to play their instruments. It wasn't for another forty-five minutes after they finished, near midnight, that the Ramones finally came on.

Something changed for me then when Joey in his ripped-up jeans and rose-colored glasses spread his legs and pressed the mike to his mouth and they ripped into an ass-kicking prototype of their as yet unreleased next hit—twenty twenty twenty-four hours to go, I wanna be sedated. It smoked. It sizzled. It was over in about a minute. But before the feedback had even faded the bassist (Dee Dee he turned out to be) screamed One Two Three Four and they hammered into "Blitzkrieg Bop" (I didn't know the titles then, of course, and couldn't understand many of the words, but in later years I would listen over and over to the studio versions and re-create that sliver of the night in my mind). It was worth the extortionary price I paid for the tickets, worth sitting through hours of white noise, worth this uncomfortable stonewalling with Jessi, who apparently I would not be seeing much of anymore. But just then for that moment I had the first and maybe best punk band in history not ten yards from me, and they were on and I had discovered something real and concrete, a new music, the vista of punk, which I think now on looking back was not only the most honest and straightforward of all the genres of that tenuous posttraumatic pulse-taking self-conscious polyester era but also the most apt commentary on it. I'd seen some shows over the years as I said, probably as many as thirty of them, from Aerosmith to Zep, but as the band segued from "Blitzkrieg" into the sensitive and insightful "Sheena Is A Punk Rocker," I knew, even then, even inside the moment, that this was the zenith, that I had found rock-and-roll deliverance in a weirdo barn-lounge somewhere in the wasteland east of the east side.

Then Jessi stood up and said something. She said it loudly so I'd be sure and hear.

I said, "What?"

"I'm leaving!"

"Where?"

"Bye!"

She pushed off between the tables and went down the risers into the screaming air-punching crowd and Joey and Tommy and Dee Dee and Richie were on fucking fire as they bashed from "Sheena" into "Teenage Lobotomy" (now I guess I'll have to tell 'em, that I got no cerebellum) and what was I going to do, let her walk off into the night and get hit over the head by some east side punk? Shit, I thought. "Shit!" I said. Some leather chick at the next table shrugged in commiseration.

At the steel door the bouncer eyeballed me and I knew I wasn't getting back in. Then I was in the cool of a midsummer night, the noise behind me fading into the distance of history as Jessi stalked off toward my car, which I'd parallel parked along the main drive because there were no regular spaces left by the time we got there. I thought at first that the night was weirdly silent until I realized it was just that I couldn't hear anything.

I caught up to her and unlocked the passenger door and went around and got in. I looked at her. She said something.

"What?"

"I want to go home!"

"You were so excited about it. About seeing them."

"I was excited about a lot of things!"

"You're mad at me."

"Oh, god, Syd—"

"I didn't call you. I'm sorry."

She shook her head.

"Jessi—"

"It's not that," she said.

"It's me," I said. Or shouted.

"It's everything! My parents are horrible. They hardly even talk to me anymore. And when they do they accuse me of having sex. With you! And we don't do anything! You don't even touch me! It's so stupid!" She leapt back out of the car and bolted into the driveway just as another car came tearing in. Stones flew as it braked and I thought for sure she was hit but somehow it missed her, apparently by turning and coming right alongside my car so fast and close that it smacked the door Jessi'd left open—my passenger door—and wrapped it clear around so it now touched the front fender. Then everything got quiet again.

The car backed away from mine with a rending shriek of unfusing metal. The guy who got out from behind the wheel looked at my door and said, "Oh, shit, man. I'm fucking sorry." He had long blond hair, I remember, pretty hair, and he staggered sideways, then leaned back against my rear fender because he was too drunk really to hold himself up. Jessi was there now in the driveway again, staring, hands over her mouth. The bouncer wandered over.

"Can you call the police?" Jessi asked him.

"Private property," he said. "They won't do nothing."

"Are you okay?" I asked her. She nodded.

"I'm really fucking sorry," the blond guy said.

The bouncer helped me pull the door back around, creaking and moaning, until, heaving against it, we were able to snap it back far enough that the latch caught and held it more or less closed.

"Don't try and open it again," the bouncer said.

"Yeah, thanks," I told him.

"I am really *really* fucking sorry," the blond guy said. He leaned into his car, then brought something over and handed it to me. It was, of all things, half an eight pack of Little Kings.

He said, "I don't need it no more."

I thanked him.

Jessi got in through my door and crawled across. I made sure she put the belt on. Even as we were pulling out I swear I could hear Joey singing "Now I wanna sniff some glue," or maybe it was just a little voice in my head.

Jessi opened two of the beers. We drove and drank (breathing recovering settling) until she said, "Where are we going?"

"You said you wanted to go home."

"I don't want to."

So I drove us around out there on the dirt roads (somewhere actually in the general vicinity of where I'd nearly killed her a month earlier), drinking the beers, until she said she was starting to feel a little carsick again and could I stop? I found a rutted turnoff into some trees, a farmer's tractor access or something, and bumped in a little ways. It was about as perfectly dark as you can get in the real world. We sat for a few moments before she said, "I am so sorry about your car. And leaving—"

"It's all right," I said. "Really. I've been shitty. I know. I deserved it."

"No. Don't say that."

"I've just been—"

"Busy. I know. You have summer school and work and I'm just this bored spoiled girl and I am so sorry about everything."

"No," I said. "I'm really the one who should apologize."

We were both quiet again. And then as if it had been agreed upon or some voiceless signal passed between us we lurched toward each other and met over the parking brake, met and began tearing, she at my clothing and I at hers. It was a lot of tearing and there were those very nice breasts involved and lips, too, and finally it required my showing her how to put the seat back all the way as I opened the glove compartment and dug out the last of those stupid condoms I'd bought at Freddy Garvey's Gulf station, and my crawling over her and sort of kneeling on the floor so I wasn't crushing her, and then me touching her, touching her and kissing her and showing her in some awkward front-seat way my version of how it was supposed to be and finally me lifting up and pressing against her as she made quiet sounds in her throat, a muted held-in crying out, and instead of just fucking her as I imagined she had been fucked, I stopped and held myself up. I thought I could make it decent, I could make it good, or at least I thought I could make it last. But it didn't last, not at all. It was over in a high school minute.

In her driveway, she leaned against me. I wondered what she felt about what had happened. I felt mostly confused. It had never been my plan to do in actuality what I pretended to have done for her parents' benefit. And I'd never had any desire to make her pay for their temerity and exploitiveness but now I knew I had, or would when it came to its inevitable end. And I had to ask myself—had I done it because of what Ted did to me, to invert the tables yet again, simply because I could? Or had it been something else between us, Jessi and me, some growing thing fed by angst and relief and sadness?

What was strange was that I slept hard that night for the first time in weeks, for the first time really since Ted figured out I wasn't doing anything to his daughter and so gleefully rubbed my face in it.

And having slept hard I awoke early enough that the birds were still singing, clawed my way up and out of bed and into some shorts and ran. The world felt new and unfolded and wet and I could smell the fecundity of summer—sap and spores and rich rotting humus. There are certain scents I have always associated with running, as if somehow the olfactory senses are awakened or sharpened by the quickened flow of body fluids. I came back glowing because even that early it was already over eighty and was supposed to hit ninety-five by midday.

On my return, Brigman and Chloe were standing in the driveway, coffee mugs in hand, inspecting my mangled passenger door. Across the street Donny pretended to work under the hood of the Road Runner.

"You get clipped or backed into?" Brigman said when I ran up.

"Hit." Sweat ran off my chin and elbows and nose. I gave a somewhat edited version of events.

"You get information?"

"No."

"Plates?"

"No."

"Fuck, Syd," he said, "you can get insurance for this."

"I can fix it," said Donny. He'd slipped over and stood now at our periphery, eyeballing the damage (which he'd obviously been over to look at earlier) and Brigman at the same time, ready to run if Brigman lashed out, but Brigman simply ignored him. "Paint it, too," Donny said.

Chloe smiled and motioned him closer. He took a sliding step in her direction.

I said, "They said the cops wouldn't come because it was private property."

"You can still file a claim," said Brigman. "There witnesses?"

"Yeah."

He looked off in frustration at my dimness.

Chloe said, "Jessi got the number."

He said, "Who?"

I said, "How do you know?"

"She called while you were running."

"You talked to her?"

"Oh, my god. I talked to Syd's girlfriend."

"She is not my girlfriend."

"She got the license?" Brigman said.

"I can do it cheap," said Donny. "Bank the insurance."

Chloe said, "She has like a photographic memory or some-thing, I guess. Did you know that?"

I said, "Why the hell did you talk to her?"

"Why the hell shouldn't I?"

"Lucky for you she did," said Brigman.

"Change that shitty color if you want, too," said Donny.

"Shit," I said.

Chloe said, "What's wrong with you? She seems nice. Funny, too."

"Funny about what?"

"What an asshole you are." They all laughed, even Donny, then she said, "Kidding. I think she really likes you."

It was barely ten o'clock and sweltering, and I felt frozen. I didn't know what to do with her now, didn't know what I'd done.

"So," Donny said, "you want me to start on it?"

Brigman turned as if he had only then registered Donny's presence and said, "What are you doing over here?"

Donny moved his mouth a little but nothing came out.

"You don't have no business here, do you?"

"I can fix it."

"*I* can fuckin fix it."

"And paint it? You can't paint it. You ain't even got the equip-ment."

"I can have it fucking painted, Donny," Brigman said. "Go away."

"*Stop* it," Chloe said. Brigman pointed at her but she didn't let him get started. "Don't tell me to shut up," she said. "You don't have to treat him like dirt just because you think you know something. You don't know anything."

"Chloe—" he said.

"Hey," I said. "Donny. I'll talk to you about it later. All right? Maybe we can do something."

"Shut up, Syd," Brigman said.

"*You* shut up," said Chloe. He froze. We all froze, but I'm not sure if it was because of the words or her look that stopped us, because it was exactly the look my mother gave. I'd forgotten it really until I saw it, saw her, in Chloe's face like that. It was kind of scary, a thing Chloe had never conjured up before, but here it was now, here she was, our mother incarnate.

Then Brigman unfroze and said, "What'd you say to me?" and I could hear him saying it to Sandy, remembered him saying it to her in exactly that voice, that tone, and remembered the feeling that something had just precipitated out that was maybe going to poison us, felt in fact that same prickling in my upper spine I'd felt as a kid when I knew they were going to fight.

"You heard me."

"Don't you ever—"

"It's my life," she said.

"Not yet, it's not."

"It is. And I'll do what I want. *See* who I want."

"Not under my roof."

"Well," she said calmly, as if some decision had been reached, "if that's how you want it." And she turned and walked deliberately, careful to show no anger, into the house.

To Donny, Brigman said, "Happy?"

"I'll talk to you about the car, Donny," I said.

"Really?"

I nodded.

"Okay, Syd," he said and tripped back across the street. I expected Brigman to rip into me but he just stared at the ground.

"She said he told you what was going on with them, that they were going out."

"Just that. I known for a long time, Syd. And it's my fault."

"What is?"

"What they been doing."

"But what is that, Brigman?"

"You know."

"*How* do you know?"

"Jesus, Syd, I caught her, more'n once. When she was just still little." And his eyes filled and his shoulders and belly moved in the tight painful clutchings of what I thought then was anger and guilt but recognized only many years later as broken-heartedness. The only other time I'd seen him cry was in the hospital when Sandy finally let go.

"You caught her with Donny?"

He shook his head. "But she started spending a lot of time with him again after Sandy went, her over to his house or him up there with her, and I'd find stuff, you know, she'd leave around. I knew." But Donny was taking her off his hands, so Brigman didn't say anything and drank until he forgot it, or didn't care. He sniffed hard and breathed in to clear himself and looked down the street. Only now that she was grown had he decided apparently to make amends.

That evening despite the fact that I had to work I met Jessi for dinner and afterward followed her to Ottawa Park. It was just dark when we got there, and as I put the Datsun into park and shut the engine off, high-beam headlights came hard up behind us and stopped, filling the car with such light that I could see dust particles hanging in the air. I said, "Shit," but after a moment the car tore around, angrily almost it seemed, as if we had usurped some prime parking spot. I caught a flash of yellow as it passed.

"That was weird," Jessi said. We walked (me carrying a blanket) and found a spot on a hillside again and this time we accomplished what we had not there before. It was easy this time—despite my misgivings and doubts and confusion the deed had already been done and doing it again felt natural. Unlike in my car it lasted this time, and when she finally cried out, viscerally, primally, in a way I had not imagined her ever sounding (such abandon! such release!), and wrapped her legs around mine and squeezed me to her, pulled me in as far as she could, it not only surprised me but sent me over along with her, and the coming seemed to last and last for us both as we strained there in the darkness each into the other. Afterward, as we lay watching the stars and the pre-Fourth drive-in pyrotechnics on the horizon I'm sure I made some lame crack about making her see fireworks.

Later, I said, "Chloe said you got that guy's license plate."

"I did."

"Thank you."

"At least it makes up for some of it."

"It wasn't your fault—"

"Syd."

"What?"

"I just like to say it. Syd. Is that all right?"

It wasn't. But lying there in a postcoital cloud, in the air of a summer night with a young and bounteous and intelligent woman, I could not bring myself to murmur anything but a mild "Mmm," which she of course took as approval.

At our cars on that quiet park street we kissed and then I followed her to where she turned west toward the estate section and I turned toward the downtown. I was pretty much alone on that middle-city road when these bright lights lit me up again. They appeared so suddenly and so close that the only possibility was that the driver had come up on me with his lights off. For the first time, perhaps because I was alone now, I felt fear.

Though I sped up, pushed the Datsun to sixty-five, hoping for a cop to pull me over, my pursuer had no trouble keeping his bumper in tight proximity to mine. Under a streetlight I saw yellow in my mirror as I had before.

There was no one behind us that I could see, so I hit my brakes. My car was already ruined—let this one hit me, too. But he didn't hit me. He stopped as short as I did. He was good. And then we sat there, looking at each other. I couldn't make out his face. Another car came up behind him and honked, then tore around us. I watched it, and when I looked back, the yellow car was gone. But I understood.

It was how Ted knew nothing was happening between me and Jessi when he'd been so happy at the hospital that morning. He'd hired someone, who I heard on the golf course that night, and who, when he heard me refusing Jessi, reported that back. But now on this evening he had seen something very different and so after harassing me was surely phoning his boss. So Ted knew already, almost as soon as I did, that it was not nothing happening between his daughter and me anymore.

PART FOUR

They got a name for the winners in the world
I want a name when I lose

—STEELY DAN (1978)

THIRTEEN

On the morning of Wednesday, the Fourth of July, I slept after work and the moment I got up Chloe met me in the hallway to say that Jessi had called.

"Hey," she said, when I reached her, "if you're not doing any-thing today, come over. Bring your swimming suit."

"Really?"

"Bring your sister, too."

"Chloe?"

"Do you have any others?"

"No."

"Then her."

"Your parents—"

"Don't worry. Just come over."

Like a weakling, like a fool, like the sadist I was becoming, I said, "Sure." I hung up and clutched at my stomach, sickened at the obscenity of how happy she sounded, and somehow blaming Ted for all of it.

"What'd she want?" Chloe said. She'd been listening.

"We're going swimming."

From the spuriously cavalier manner in which she said, "Cool,"

I knew that Jessi had asked her already when they'd talked the first time.

It was the largest backyard swimming pool I'd ever seen (I would learn later that it was actually one of the largest private pools in the entire country at that time), the size of a basketball court it seemed to me, with two black lane lines painted on the bottom on one side of it and separated on the surface by a string of orange floats. I'd never been back here before, never seen it up close (and never realized the full extent of the grounds as they extended back through foliage so heavy and deep you couldn't begin to see beyond it—it was at least two acres, I figured, right in the middle of the city). The pool itself was constructed of thousands of aqua and navy tiles, and surrounded by a broad apron of concrete that burned white in the sun. A stainless steel whirlpool off the shallow end whirred and chugged. At the rear stood two redwood-shingle-sided structures, one a cabana with sliding glass doors and the other (Jessi told us), much the smaller of the two, a cedar sauna.

I had seen neither hair nor hook of Joyce and Ted and assuaged myself with the supposition that they must not be around, that their absence (perhaps even another out-of-town trip?) was all that Jessi had meant when she said not to worry—T and J were away, so the kids could play. I even relaxed a little, floated on an inflatable raft and watched the deep clear sky.

The recommended itinerary, Jessi instructed us, was to swim first, get your muscles warmed up and your skin cooled down, then to run into the sauna where the steam would pull the impurities from your now nicely circulating blood. The effect of walking into that matrix of humidity, that gelatinous air, and the overpowering scent of cedar immediately upon leaving the water was dizzying. Benches ran around the entire perimeter and it was a good thing because I think I'd have fallen down if I'd had to stand. I opened my mouth and gasped fish-like, pulled at the thickness and heat of it, and felt the pores of the skin of all my body open and weep. Chloe and Jessi sat opposite me, across the raised central bed of heated lava rocks, and close enough together that they could speak without my really hearing them over the hissing. Every so often Jessi lifted a ladle full of water from a built-in steel bowl beneath a faucet and poured it on the rocks, which hissed all the more loudly. (As I watched the two of them talk I felt frankly surprised at Chloe. I imagined her cooing and oohing over every rich-person knick and knack in this wonderland, Car and Dog and Persian Rug and Microwave Oven, etc., but she acted as if she were a secret heiress and this was all pleasant but not any real big deal. She dived without comment into the mammoth pool, hung on the edge chatting with Jessi, sunned herself, then lounged in the sauna as if she'd been going every day for years. And not an awed or ogling or covetous gawkish-teenage-working-class comment about any of it beyond a polite thank-you-for-inviting-me to Jessi when we arrived.) It seemed an hour in the steam, though it was only probably ten minutes before the girls stood and I followed them, blinded by sweat and light, into the relative crispness of the day.

"Don't wait!" Jessi commanded. "Dive!"

And she did and Chloe did, and so I did, and the shock of that seeming iciness, of such a rapid reduction in my body temperature, again made me wonder if I was about to lose consciousness (it was beginning to occur to me that I might not have the constitution to be wealthy). I came up in the sloping netherworld between the shallow end and the deep, shook the water from my face as I trod, then found the bottom with my toes, and looked around at Jessi and Chloe sitting on the edge already, thigh to thigh. Only then did I notice the bathing-suited foursome walking toward us, towels over arms—it was the Mastersons, Dotty-'n-Dave, and their hosts, the Mr. and Mrs. Ted Kesslers—and feel my scrotum shrivel even more than it already had.

"Halloo!" old Masterson shouted.

Jessi turned and waved and set about introducing Chloe. Ted nodded and gave her his left hand to shake, then walked around toward the sectioned-off lanes. You could see the whole apparatus of his artificial arm now, the almost flesh-colored plastic that fitted up over his stump and the cables and wires that allowed him somehow to control the hook. Except now the hook was gone, replaced (or covered) by a kind of paddle. For swimming, of course. I wondered how many different attachments he had for the various activities of his weird life. As I watched (without him so much as glancing at me) he began turning laps.

Joyce stood at the pool's edge for several moments shading her eyes, watching Ted and me, I suppose, in the water together. Then she said, "Hello, Syd," and dived.

She slid beneath the surface toward me, her image rippled from the refraction of the water (even beneath that wavering surface I could make out the swell of her black-Speedo-clad bottom) so that I thought for a moment we were going to collide. In that tiny moment—Ted swimming oblivious, Jessi and Chloe turned away talking to the Mastersons—Joyce and I were alone among them. And she must have been as aware of it as I was (or more frighteningly she wasn't) for as she glided alongside me, still beneath the surface, so close that I felt her hair brush my thigh, she reached over, placed her hand on the front of my bathing suit and squeezed me firmly enough that I nearly doubled over, but at the same time sweetly, if that's possible. Lovingly, even.

Later that very holiday afternoon, after the spread of deli meats and cheeses and buns and toppings and salads and iced beers laid out on the glass table in the glass porch (Chloe still acting as if this were all old hat), after Chloe and Jessi slipped up to Jessi's room for some serious girl talk and the Mastersons and Ted retired, scotches in hand, to the woody library, I took a Molson back out to the whirlpool. I was sipping and soaking contentedly, eyes closed, when I sensed something and looked up to find Joyce, still in her Speedo, watching me. She squatted and reached for my beer, which I handed her, took a sip, handed it back, and then got in. She sat on the seat for a moment, then slipped to the floor so that the water came up to her chin.

"So, how are you, Syd?" she said.

"Passable."

"Only passable. It could be so much better, couldn't it?"

"I guess that depends on what you want it to be better than."

"Jessi had a talk with us."

"Did she?"

"She thinks it's getting serious between you two." I wondered what she knew, if she and Ted talked much anymore. "It's time to stop, don't you think? Or are you trying to hurt her, too?"

"No."

She got back on the seat and lay her arm along the edge so that her fingers just reached my shoulder, and stroked me there. "I've been miserable, Syd. I miss you. Does that upset you, that you haven't made me hate you yet? That I want to touch you? Does that disappoint you?"

"Or maybe that you're having me followed?"

"What?"

"Tell me you don't know about it."

She shook her head. She said, "I have to say I'm not surprised. He's done it to me."

"I thought that was the point."

"Before, I mean. He hired people to watch me, photograph me. He even had them set me up. I was out with some friends once, girls' night out, and this guy kept hitting on me. So finally I danced with him. It was no big deal, believe me. Later Ted produced pictures and a tape recording and tried to make out like I'd been the one coming on."

"So—why do you do it now? I mean for him."

"In the beginning I hated it. Hated him for it. But once the secret was out, that he'd watched me, he kept bringing it up. He wanted to talk about it, ask me questions. What I felt like with other men. Did I find them attractive? Did it turn me on when they hit on me? He got off on it, knowing other men wanted his wife.

"So, I made things up—a man touched me or I felt drawn to someone. It drove him crazy. We started going to bars and sitting apart so he could watch men buy me drinks. I didn't do anything with them, just talked. In the beginning it didn't take much. We'd just have a drink, then I'd meet Ted outside and it was all he could do to get home before—sometimes we didn't make it home. Eventually he wanted to see me with someone else."

"And so I wandered in."

"No. There were others. Not videotaped, though."

"You mean he watched? Secretly?"

"But it drove him crazy. What he really wanted was to have something, possess something, a trophy."

"Weren't there—couldn't you find someone, you know, to just do it with him there?"

"It was never about the sex itself. It's always about control. Power. His owning it. His owning this other person, and me. If he just participated, then he wouldn't own anything. It would just be sex. He'd be equal to us."

"Christ."

"I don't want to talk about it anymore. I just want you to touch me again."

"So you can tell him?"

Her mouth tightened and her eyes grew big and moist, then she got out and retreated to the cabana. It had drapes across the sliding glass door but she did not pull them and did not close the door. She stood to the side of the opening so that I could see her but someone looking from the house could not and peeled her suit down from one breast, then the other, and pushed it to her feet and knew exactly what it was doing to me under the foaming water, stood waiting for the part of me that wanted terribly to go to her and lift her up right there against the wall. Then someone came out of the house—it was Jessi and Chloe. When I looked back at the cabana, Joyce had pulled the drapes.

*　　*　　*

The girls wanted to see fireworks. I suggested one of the drive-ins that still shot them off but they insisted on a park out of the city that supposedly had the biggest display in the county. I had to work but Jessi said we could both drive, then she'd take Chloe home. A little later I whispered to Chloe not to let Jessi in the house. She just gave me her "do-I-really-look-that-stupid?" look.

We'd been there fifteen minutes, with about that long to go until it would be dark enough for the show to start, when Donny walked up, hands in pockets and a glow in his cheeks. He said, with as much verve and linguistic invention as I had ever heard him muster, "Hey, you guys."

"Oh," said Chloe and jumped up and was going to kiss him, but thought better of it and just took his hands in hers. She said to Jessi, "This is Donny."

I regarded the three of them, feeling well and truly set up. None of this had anything to do with fireworks, at least not of the pyrotechnic variety.

"You think you know what you're doing?" I asked Jessi.

She smiled, shyly, slyly, and blinked those big bang-battered black-framed peepers. When I grunted, she took my hand, the romance of the moment just about overwhelming all of us. We watched the sky for the first ascending trails of light and the explosions they portended.

I smoked two cigarettes on the way back, daring Ted's follower to come up behind me again and trembling to visions of my Other Self locking it up, then leaping out to pummel him. But nothing happened, and the hospital was pretty quiet for a Fourth of July. I didn't get called to the ER until after one, and then only for a routine draw—liver enzymes for a rule-out hepatitis. The main trauma suites at the front were sectioned off from each other by drapes but the smaller treatment rooms had hard partitions, thin walls and doors, to afford the conscious a little privacy. I went in to find a middle-aged man, beefy and big-headed and balding, with thick darkly hairy forearms that lay on the sheet covering him. He had the slightest amber cast about him. A common scenario in a case like this was a junkie who'd got a dirty spike but this guy had nothing like the pallid emaciated look most of them did. The opposite, in fact. He looked like he could have broken one of them in two. Maybe an experimenter, they try it not knowing what they're doing and end up here, jaundiced and with a swollen gut.

He watched me. He said, "Close the door, will you, pal?" It was a bit of an unusual request but I kicked the door shut. When I approached him, he looked at my ID badge, then said my name, "Daniel Redding. So you want to stick me."

"That's the idea."

"Enjoy it while you got the chance."

"What?"

He put his arm out and balled a big hard fist.

"Relax it," I said, and tied on the rubber and put the needle in. He didn't flinch and had no problem watching the blood come, so again I thought maybe he'd been needle experimenting, but his arms were as clean as mine.

"Sticking people all you do for a living?"

"Such as it is," I told him.

When I'd taken the needle out, he held the cotton to the puncture and said, "I thought they called you Syd."

I looked at him and said, "Who are you?"

"Ah," he said.

"You work here or something?"

"Well, I don't work here. But I'm working."

I wanted suddenly to get out of there. I said, "Whatever," and cut the needle and picked up my tray.

"Don't get snotty."

Maybe they should've added a lithium level to the enzymes. I'd ask the doc on the way out. Then the guy said, "Syd, the child-fucker."

My scalp tightened. I thought to move but didn't, as if what was happening was too fascinating for me to budge from it.

"You know who I am?" he asked.

"No."

"Sure you do. I drive a VW Rabbit. Yellow. Quick little thing, isn't it?"

"I'm going to get security."

"Pansy-asses. Whyn't you call the real cops? Or let me. I know plenty of 'em. Used to be one, in fact. Let me tell you something, you horny little prick—" I shook my head. I was so shaken and angry and confused and frightened I felt like just screaming at him, but I only stood there. "—starting now, Jessi Kessler is off limits to you."

"You piece of shit," I said, while making the concurrent mistake of stepping toward him, which was when his hand shot out and he grabbed my package, my jewels, so tightly that the breath was propelled from me and I could only let out a kind of wheezing grunt. I dropped the tray (the vacuum tubes cracking and imploding) and sagged, but he held me up. The needle hole opened and a thick line of blood ran down across his forearm.

"Watch your mouth, lover boy, and don't fuck with me. You want to play rough, I'll teach you some things but I'm giving you this warning first, and that's all this is—a warning. Knock it off. Leave her alone."

He let go, and it was all I could do not to drop to my knees. He swung his legs over and stood up. He was as short as he was thick but looked down at me because I was bent over, holding myself, trying to breathe, and said, "Oh, you can throw that blood out. There's nothing wrong with me."

I looked up at him.

"I took a pill to turn me yellow, so they'd be sure and call you up here."

*   *   *

I skipped Physics in the morning and went home but only slept until noon. For a moment when I woke up I was able to convince myself that the damage had healed. Then I moved. It had dulled, though, from a sharpness in which I could feel my heart beat into something deeper and achier. If I adjusted my stride a little I could walk without charges shooting down my legs as they had for the remainder of the night. (At one point Phyllis told me I didn't look well and offered to let me go home, but I said no. Thankfully the night stayed slow.) I put in toast and was frying an egg when the front door bell rang and then I heard the door opening before I could answer it.

I stopped in the archway to the living room. In the midst of all of Brigman's trash stood Joyce. It was the oddest sensation, seeing her like that in our house—she looked too big for the place, too alive, as if it couldn't possibly hold her and had no right to try.

I said, "What are you doing?"

"I was afraid you'd turn me away."

"Other people live here, you know."

"They left. I saw them." They'd both gone to work. (Chloe was full time now. She'd turned out to be one of the best workers the Pretzel Bitch had ever hired, and had even developed a following of mall rats who waited to get their carb fix from her.)

"So now you're watching them, too?"

"No, Syd. I just didn't want to cause trouble. I wanted to surprise you."

"Well, I'm surprised."

"I meant while you were sleeping."

"That's not a good idea."

"It was never a good idea." She came across to me, picking her way between the stacks and piles.

"Why would you come here?"

"I wanted to see you."

"I mean, all this crazy shit is going on—"

"I think you're embarrassed." She looked around.

I didn't say anything.

"You think you're the only one who comes from poor? You think you know something about white trash?"

"I guess I do now."

Her eyes moistened again as they had in the Jacuzzi. "It doesn't go away, you know," she said. "You're as much proof of that as I am." Then she came closer, until we were nearly touching, and said, "I know how angry you've been. I feel that way, too, sometimes. But we can help each other." She put her hand between my legs and cupped me in a way that normally would've been nice but now, in my condition, sent out flares so that I grunted and bent forward.

"Something wrong?"

"I . . . hurt myself," I said.

She said, "Oh," but instead of letting go, she squeezed a little harder. She said, "Do you understand what I mean, about helping each other?"

At first I didn't but she squeezed harder still, so that I could hardly breathe, and then I found I did understand. I felt not only a kind of reactive indignation at the pain but a concurrent thrill as well—a dizzying rush at the deeply illicit darkness, the dirty danger she was offering up, the implicit suggestion that this was one of those tit-tat deals, the old give-and-get—that I had not felt before even with her and that immediately and thoroughly intoxicated me. I reached around with my free hand and slid my fingers into her hair, made a fist and tightened it and looked down into her upturned face, the opened mouth, the breath coming hard now as she held me so tightly that the pain had turned white. I twisted her hair until she cried out, then opened my mouth and lowered it onto hers.

FOURTEEN

Masterson called to tell me about an undergraduate fellowship that had just opened up in the fall down in Columbus, at Ohio State. It was a one-semester deal where you'd live in a dorm, take some classes, and also work as an assistant in a cancer research lab. Most of the cost would be covered by a grant, but we'd need to get off an application right away if I was interested.

"It would beef up your credentials," he said. "Look great on your apps. Think about it. Oh, and you'll need a letter of reference, too, of course. I was talking to Dr. Kessler this morning so I took the liberty of mentioning it to him."

"What'd he say?"

"He said he'd consider it. You'll need to ask him yourself, though."

I told him thanks and said I'd stop in and fill out the forms.

Then, as if I had drifted somehow into a parallel world of normalcy and plain work, a chunk of time (the week of mid-terms) slipped past during which I laid eyes on no Kessler. It was, I guess, my summer vacation. Jessi and I agreed that I would just go through it with my head down, and then we'd have the rest of the summer, at least until finals week and she had to leave for Cleveland. Joyce did not come over again. I think she was waiting for me to make contact this time, but she would've known of my exams. I took some vacation days for cramming and so only worked one night that week, and on that morning Ted was late, which allowed me to take the chicken's way out vis-à-vis the letter request—I left a note on his desk. I was obligated to ask because of Masterson (who knew nothing, of course, of any of this weirdness) but figured that this way Ted could just ignore it and we could avoid another messy face-to-face. I hadn't seen him since his goon accosted me in the ER and didn't know what might come out of my mouth.

But I thought about them, and they each appeared regularly in my dreams. And I thought about just not going back over, about letting it all go. Surely at that point I could have called it even, and just as surely the possibility of any further benefit from Ted had long since been ruined. Jessi would be gone in the fall, anyway. It'd hurt her, and maybe Joyce, but wouldn't the pain be greater the longer things continued? Or was that it—that my vengefulness was not yet satisfied? I admit that when Ted gnashed his teeth or Joyce teared up or Jessi whined it satisfied some small black spot in my heart.

But it was also true that I'd come to care for Jessi, had moved perhaps into that dangerous land of affection, that Joyce left a vacuum in my gut, an ever-present hunger, and that my always fermenting hatred of Ted ran so hot after this latest incident that it constituted a kind of sentimental attachment. I'd even come to feel some fondness for that stupid little beast Dog, and he in turn, probably precisely because I'd always been cold and distant, refusing to coo and pet like the rest of them, had taken to celebrating my arrivals by promptly peeing on the floor at my feet, then rolling on his back and spreading his legs.

As specious as it sounds, I held a kind of power over an entire family of wealthy, intelligent, beautiful beings. And since I had apparently now forgone any real chance of becoming like them (successful, that is), perhaps that explains as well as anything my inability to quit. I think I could have walked away from entanglements with any one of them, but all together? I was not that strong. So, power? Was that why I stayed, and what led to the remarkable events that would come to pass in the remainder of that summer? Perhaps. Though, on writing it, I must say that it looks not quite right. Love, I think, with all its contradictions and inconsistencies and the precarious place it occupies just across that old thin line from you-know-what, comes closer.

On that Saturday, after a hard night, the phone woke me.

"I'm sorry," Jessi said. "Chloe said you'd be up by now."

"I was," I said, trying to sound awake. I felt frozen in my stupor; I didn't know what to do with her now, in the space this distance had opened, where it stood or what I'd done or what would happen anymore if I kept doing it.

"Come over?" she said. "Just for a little while?"

It stung, how she said that—so buoyed by us, so hungry. The thought of breaking it off with her made my stomach clutch, and not just because it would hurt her. I missed her. It occurred to me then what she'd said.

"Did you say Chloe?"

"Hmm? Will you come?"

"Maybe."

"Dinnertime? I'll make you something."

"You cook?"

"Melted cheese globs and beer. You know that."

"Mmm. Your parents, though—"

"Things are different."

"Did you have another talk with them?"

"What?"

I waited. My face felt hot.

She said, "You said 'another' talk."

"Did I?"

"Yes. But I never told you I talked with them."

"You must have."

"I know I didn't. I'm positive. I thought about telling you."

"Then I guess I assumed it. Things seemed to change at some point."

I could hear her clicking something against the phone. She said, "What would I have said to them?"

"I don't know. That I was psychotic and if they weren't nice to me I might do something really crazy."

"That was it," she said. "You must have a spy here."

"Dog and I talk."

"Come over?"

"All right."

Ted opened the door. He held a folded-over newspaper pinched in his hook and continued to read without ever looking at me. I offered no greeting, either, nor did I ask about the letter. Anything civil I said at that point would've been as much an affront as something nasty. And how would the conversation have gone?

Hey, Ted, that was pretty good, hiring a thug to squeeze my nuts. I mean, you really got me there.

Thanks, Syd. He does nice work. Tell him I said hey, won't you, next time when he beats the shit out of you?

I found my way through the dining room and kitchen and sun porch to the back where they—I counted four heads in the pool—floated or splashed and shouted.

"Hey, you," Jessi said, and then another of the bobbers, who turned out to be Chloe, lifted an arm and waved, and then the third. "Heya, Syd," said Donny. Joyce did not wave but watched me walk toward them.

"Get on your suit," said Jessi. I nodded but sat in one of the row of rubber-slatted aluminum-tube-framed deck chairs. As I sat watching them play I grew . . . well, I wanted to get mad. It felt justified. You can see what'd happened—that the week or so of my and Jessi's separation had been filled for her by a surrogate,

my sister. And in turn, she, Chloe, had been granted a haven, a little love-nest sanctuary in which she could see as much of her ban-
ished boyfriend as she wanted. But I didn't feel mad. Tired,
maybe. Sad. A little dumbfounded at how prodigiously I had mis-
managed things, let them slip away from whatever modicum of
control I once had over them. But it all seemed such a smooth
continuum—this led to that and now here I sat watching these
four inhabitors of my life cavort together.

" 'Bout your car?" Donny said.

"I'm still thinking."

"You all right?" It was Jessi.

I nodded.

"Come on in."

I shook my head.

"You're not all right. What's wrong?"

"Just tired."

"You want to lie down?"

"I don't know." I stood up.

"Where are you going?"

"Talk to your dad."

"Oh," she said. She looked as surprised as I felt at having said it.
The notion came to me that I might still turn it back, call the whole
thing off, return to Ted his daughter and his wife, and then grovel
to try to resurrect my future. I went to the library and from the window glimpsed his car backing down the driveway hard enough that
you could tell he was all mad again. Probably going to meet the ex-
cop, have a couple of drinks and figure out what to do to me next.

"Did he leave?" Joyce had come up behind me wrapped in a
towel. "Jessi said you don't feel well."

"I'm fine."

"Are you still having pain?"

"No. A little."

"Are you angry?"

"I don't know."

"Come."

I followed her back to the kitchen. She stood at the sink, facing the window, which looked out through the sun room to the backyard where we could see the three others.

"I should go be sociable," I said. "I mean, I came over to see her."

"You didn't come over to see her. That's why you're angry."

"It is?"

"Get rid of it, Syd."

"I'm not—"

"Touch me."

I put my hand on her shoulder.

She said, "Ted uses a belt."

"What?"

She pushed the straps of her suit down over her shoulders, then pulled the suit down over her hips and peeled it off. She put her hands on the edge of the counter and leaned forward, legs slightly spread.

She said, "Do you like that?"

I didn't answer.

"Do it."

"Joyce—"

"Hurry up. They're coming."

Donny and Jessi were climbing out as Chloe toweled off.

"I don't—"

"Do it! Get rid of it!"

In the motion you would use to pitch a fast softball, I reached back and swung my hand forward. Her ass felt cold and dense, and the sound was stiff and muffled.

"Oh, god!" she said. "Take off your belt. Hurry."

It was an old worn canvas thing with a sliding brass buckle. I slid it off, doubled it over and cracked it against her.

"Harder!"

They were walking toward the house.

I swung again and again, whipping her especially robustly with the last few strokes, which left pink welts that I guessed would rise and darken. Only as they stepped onto the sun porch did she gather her suit and towel and look at me and say, "You're not so different, you know, the two of you," and hurry out.

I stuffed the belt in my pocket and was sitting at the table when they entered. "You okay?" Jessi asked.

I nodded.

"Hungry?"

"Starved," I said.

Later the four of us were in the kitchen, Jessi and Chloe drinking Cokes, Donny and me having a beer, when Joyce came in and started banging around. She kept looking at me (though I don't think the others noticed). At one point she even motioned with her head toward the door—she wanted to see me outside. I pretended not to get it, and when I held Jessi's hand on the table, Joyce glared at me (oh, it was hateful) and stalked out and slammed the door.

"Jesus," Chloe said. "What's with her?"

Jessi just rolled her eyes, as if to say, Who knows this time? We could hear the 280Z tearing down the drive.

A little later Jessi said, "Swim?" I nodded, but Chloe said no and went with Donny into a little television den off the dining room. It was dark out. I'd have to leave for work in an hour. I got my suit from the car but when I started into the cabana, Jessi, who was already in the water, said, "Don't put your suit on. I didn't." She hadn't turned on the lamps around the concrete apron or the powerful underwater spot.

"What if they come out?"

"They won't." From the way she said it I knew there was an arrangement.

I met her in mid-pool where I could just reach the bottom, and held her, and we began a kind of dance, a twirling under the warm summer night supported by the water so that even if we tipped and went under I had only to kick to right us, and she did not let me go. I felt all the parts of her against me, her breath and her breasts, her thighs and her belly, her mouth against my mouth, breathing my air, our tongues playing, teeth clicking, and ever so faintly, against the upreaching tip of my erection, the wetted wooliness between her legs, and the different slicker wetness beneath it. Sometimes she lowered herself just enough that she nipped the tip of my cock with that mouth, pulled it in a bit and let it go, and I was so hard then, so teased, that I could feel the aching remnants of the bruising.

I slipped my arms beneath her legs so that my elbows rode in the crooks of her knees and lowered her so that I penetrated her gradually and in a way over which she had no control, until I was planted and she made a sound deep in her throat. We held like that for a long time, turning still, dancing, then I raised her up again and set her down. It went on in that slow aqueous way, and even at our climax I tried not to speed up too much, and she did not move against me, so that it happened in the same slow motion as our dance, the breaking waves of it making us shudder so that we must have sent out ripples. Like fishes we spilled ourselves into the water and each other.

Then we heard a sound in the blackness at the back of the estate.

"Dog?" she said.

No answer came, and then a sound again.

"Who is it?" she said.

"Shh," I whispered, and let her go and slipped to the side and out into the cool darkness, and ran, naked and wet, and heard it again, though farther away now, because it, whatever it was, had run away.

He caught me on top of the parking garage, just about where Ted had confronted me, only he didn't want to talk. I was careless to even go up there, to follow my habits, and made it easy for him and easier still by not paying attention. I had barely stepped from my car when he came out of the shadows and swung his fist up into my gut. That suddenly I was down, airless and incapacitated.

He knelt beside me. I was on my knees, folded over. "Every time," he said. He was panting a little, though probably more from adrenaline than exertion. It's strange the things you think of when your world is wiped clean by the act of dying. "Every time you see her, I'm gonna pound your fucking ass."

I fell over onto the stained and grease-scented concrete.

"You're not too bright, so I guess this is what it's gonna take till you get it. Leave. Jessi. Kessler. The. Fuck. Alone."

My grunt must have sounded something like a response, because he stepped back and turned toward his car (the one I'd stupidly failed to notice though it was right there under a light). I managed to pull in enough air to speak, and said, or grunted, "Hey."

He turned and stood backlighted by the street lamp, so I could only make out his bulk and the shape of his ape arms bowing away from his sides.

"Don't know . . . your name."

"What?"

"If we're . . . gonna . . . meet like this—"

He laughed. He said, "You are one smart-mouthed shit, you know that? You might not be too bright, but you got balls. It's Ron."

"Ron," I said. "Seeya."

He laughed again, and left.

So began a new phase.

Under the guise of adventure—trying a restaurant in a strange part of the city; catching an afternoon movie; a day trip to anywhere—I steered Jessi into surreptitiousness. She seemed not to suspect anything. I just didn't come to the house anymore. She in fact began coming to mine afternoons when Brigman and Chloe were at work (I learned not to be self-conscious about the mess, and anyway she never commented on it, as if everyone's house looked like this), and in my room in my bed we made slow love in the way we had discovered in the pool. Her face grew pink and moist, and her lips dry. So much persisted in this way and so much was delivered that it was almost as if we had discovered some new activity altogether, our own form of physical communion that was derived from and related to sexual intercourse but had become something other than that, something new. Eventually we could last on the very edge for a full hour (I timed it on my alarm clock), and the release then was symphonic, epiphanic (it's silliness really to even suggest a word for it).

In the meantime, in Holiday Inns and Motel 6s and a by-the-hour cottage on a highway west of town, I was spanking her mother. Oh, I beat that woman's bounteous ass until it reddened and rocked, the reverberations riding down even into her dimply thighs, but not only that, no. I'd turn her over and push apart her legs and straddle her and with a limp leather strap that'd once been the belt to a 60s Chanel suit of hers whipped her there, too (that furry mons, those swollen swollen lips), until the juices flew, and I could see in her face that, whether she deserved it or not, she was in her bliss. You should know that she began then also, from that first living room moment of our reunion, to teach me about pain. I was open to it as I was open to everything she suggested if for no other reason than that I wanted still (perhaps even more desperately than before) to please her.

Even the first time she bound my wrists and ankles and blind-folded me and lit a candle and stung me with globules of hot wax, and I writhed against the restraints and swore magnificently at her, she said she knew that I was finally beginning to understand the secret: that this made it even better.

I did not plan this, did not conspire to double-time them with each other. My sin was weakness, not having the will to say no to any of it. My god, though, I have to say they both seemed happy in those middlemost weeks of summer—Jessi just lay sometimes looking at me and smiling and running her fingers over my face; Joyce took to licking me in surprising places, on the cheek or elbow or the back of my calf—and their happiness made me happy, too, at least for the hours we were together and there was no room to think of anything else but us.

In this way we passed into August.

FIFTEEN

I came home one morning to find Chloe's car idling in the street, and her in her work uniform dragging two suitcases and an overnight makeup kit down the front steps. When she huffed and set them down at the curb, I said, "Going somewhere?"

"Work."

"Long shift, huh?"

"Shut up, Syd. I'm moving out, all right? Now you can run over and tell my dad."

"You think he might not notice?"

"You're so funny."

"Maybe you should talk to him."

"I'll call him."

"Oh. Well, good."

She lifted one case into the trunk, then the other.

"Where you going to stay?" I asked then, as mildly as I could, though it was the question we'd both been waiting for.

"Jessi's."

I think I actually staggered. I said, "What do you mean?"

"Jessi? Remember her? Big house. Small dog."

"Chloe—you can't."

"She invited me." She threw in the makeup case and slammed

the lid. "It's not like they don't have the room. And *they* don't treat me like I'm twelve or something."

"Well, from what I hear about when you were twelve, that's probably a good thing."

Her face fluoresced. I braced for a lashing, but not for her leaving without another word, which is what she did. It was for some reason just then that I understood it had gone bad, all of it, and was going to come crumbling down. I just didn't know yet how bad, and how much would come.

When I pulled up at the station Brigman came out of one of the bays as if he knew already. I figured if I didn't tell him that when he found out later he'd be pissed about that, too. Plus, he couldn't really blow up at work. "Listen—" I said.

When I finished, he said, "Who are these people?"

"You know who—"

"This is your girlfriend?"

"Well—her father is that pathologist. Ted Kessler. With the one arm?"

"You're dicking around with that guy's daughter?"

"Sort of."

"How'd you manage that?"

"It's kind of a long story."

"Chloe's staying there?"

"Donny comes over, too."

"Does he stay over, too?"

"Not that I know of."

"She safe?"

"Yeah."

"Fuckin Donny, I'll kick his ass. And this doctor, who does he think he is? Maybe you should tell Jessi to move in with us, see how he likes it."

"Oh," I said, "yeah, that'd be great. If we'd just put in a pool and expand the house a little. Listen, do you want to—I could take you over there."

"Fuck it."

"She said she'd call."

"Whatever." He turned away, back to the banging and ratcheting and torquing of his life.

Jessi met me in the student union pizza bar.

She said, "I'm sorry about this—I should have at least told you. I know it's not what you want. But I feel, I don't know, like I owe it to her or something. Like *someone* owes her something."

"Because you pity her."

"That's an awful thing to say."

"Is it? I grew up with her. I know how people treat her."

"Syd—"

"Don't get upset. I'm not blaming you. I think it's nice what you're trying to do."

"She doesn't have a very easy life."

"Really? She's got a home and a car and a job and clothes and food and school. She needs a pool, too? A mansion to live in? She needs to be able to see some child molester?"

Now she looked away, through the plate glass windows, and covered her mouth with her hand. She waited some time before she spoke. "She's just staying with us for a little while. That's all. Call it a vacation. A long slumber party."

"Because you're friends."

"Yes."

"Not that you feel sorry or you think she has this horrible life or something."

"We just hang out. There aren't that many people I like to hang out with, in case you haven't noticed."

I touched her finger and she grabbed my hand and held on. I said, "And you're leaving soon, anyway."

"Syd—" My hand must have gone clammy because she let it go. "—I'm withdrawing my acceptance."

"Why?"

"You mean is it because of you? You sound so panicked."

"No."

"It's not just because of you."

"But it is some."

"More than some."

"I—it's just a hell of an opportunity to pass up. What are you going to do?"

"Take some classes here, get a job. I don't know yet, exactly. That's the point—I want to think. You're supposed to be happy about it. You're supposed to say 'Yea! Good for us.' "

"I applied for a fellowship at OSU this fall."

"Oh."

"Don't worry. Your dad's supposed to write the letter."

She actually laughed.

"Have you told your folks?"

"Not yet."

"Well, that'll be a fun time."

"I'm glad Chloe's there. They can't go totally ape. It's such a blow, you know, Daughter not going to Daddy's alma mater. It would have looked so good."

Though we'd met in a public place I frequented, I didn't give it much thought. I mean, we only talked, and then I walked her to her car and we had a quick kiss. So when that night as I drove in to work a police cruiser sped up behind me and flashed its lights, I was not apprehensive—just confused.

"Evening," the cop said, inspecting my license.

"Was I speeding?" I said.

He handed the license back without bothering to take it to his car to check it, and said to hold on. Which I did, of course, suspecting nothing, until in my mirror I watched the passenger door open and Ron step out. I thought then about taking off, futile and self-destructive as it would have been. But I waited. He'd leer, I figured. Let me see he was so important he could get cops to make stops for him. I'd just nod and go to work.

He came up along the car as the cop had but before he came even with my open window, before I could see him beside me, inserted a nightstick and, wielding it like a pool cue, waited for me to look back at him, then rammed it into my eye. He must've been a hell of a pool player. I mean it rocked me, the pain so intense that I could only sit stunned and blinded.

He leaned in and said, "Enjoy lunch, asshole? What do you think not seeing someone means? You don't want to learn a lesson in getting really hurt, you better figure it out."

In the morning Brigman said, "The hell happened to you?" It was a pretty classic shiner, like in those old Tarryton cigarette commercials (I'd rather fight than switch!), encompassing the entire orbital from the round crown of cheekbone below to the rim above. Plus, for a little added drama, I'd had some bleeding in the eye itself, so the sclera now had a kind of scarletty vampire effect. Phyllis insisted that someone in the ER look at it, though they determined there was no internal damage. My vision was a little blurred but would come back, they thought, when the swelling went down (which it did within a day or two).

I said, "Door jumped out at me."

"Bullshit."

"What?"

"You didn't hit no door. You'd have a line. I did it once. That's round," he said, pointing, "and it went in your eye."

"What're you, a forensic expert now?"

"A what?"

"Nothing. I'm all right. I had it checked out."

"You don't want to say what happened, then don't."

I looked at him. I could feel my mouth set in the way he always set his, tight and flat to telegraph disgust or at least displeasure not just with an individual but the whole world. I said, "It was a cop's billy club," and was conscious even as I said it of how easy it was to push the Destruct button, how simple at the moment of the doing it was to change your life.

"I said fine. Don't tell me."

"It was."

"A cop hit you?"

"Ex-cop. He does surveillance and threats and stuff."

"What are you talking about?"

"Guy's been following me."

"Why?"

"Because Dr. Kessler doesn't like it that I'm going out with Jessi."

"So he hired a guy?"

"Yeah."

"And he *hits* you?"

"He has a few times."

He lifted his beer from the TV tray and drank and set it back, all the while not taking his eyes off me.

"Why'n the hell wouldn't you say nothing?"

Because even now his face was reddening in the way I had seen it only a few times—and never since the wreck—not with a temper flare, which was common with him, but a true burn, a dangerous thing. Because it wasn't his mess. Because I didn't want to have to talk about any of it.

Once at Motorhead a guy said some things to him low enough that I couldn't hear, but I didn't need to. I watched Brigman's face in the bonfire light and felt the heat coming off him hotter than the fire, and I knew the guy needed to shut up and go, but he was drunk and he kept on. I've wondered since what he was saying, or rather who it was about, because I could think of nothing else that would set Brigman off in that way other than an insult to someone he cared about. I mean, if you bad-mouthed his car, he'd just tell you let's drive. I never figured out who the guy was, but I knew before it happened what was going to. I wasn't even sure until later that I saw it it was so quick. Brigman put his left hand around behind the guy's head, almost like he was giving him a hug, their faces close together. Brigman said something, and the guy seemed to laugh, and then that fast Brigman brought the guy's head down and his own knee up and the guy was on the ground bleeding and screaming, his nose spread up across his forehead. Brigman pointed at me to follow and we were gone. No repercussions that I knew of ever came from it.

But I felt glad now, too, that he knew. I was scared. I wanted this guy off me, wanted something on my side other than my big mouth.

"You know his name?"

"Ron," I said.

"I want Chloe home."

As if she'd been expecting company Joyce answered the door in a rich-suburban-doctor's-wife getup—black slacks and a sort of tunic in a quasi-African print (zebra stripes on a gold background) held by a gold chain-link belt, jewelry on the neck and wrists and ears, makeup and perfume. I lost my composure for a moment and just looked at her, and she, fixed on my eye, looked back. We stood like that until I said, "Hello, Mrs. Kessler. I wondered if I could have my sister back?"

I thought she'd laugh, but she only glared, as she had that night in the kitchen. She said, "You'd better come in." In the foyer she inspected my face from several angles, palpated the bruise until I winced, but instead of asking what happened, she said, "Jessi tells us she's not going to Case."

"Oh."

She regarded me, then said, "Does this make you happy, Syd?"

"No. I think she should go. I told her that."

"Well, maybe you'd better do something more than just tell her."

"I thought it was Ted who wanted her to go so badly."

"We both do. Though maybe for different reasons." She smiled now, for the first time, and put her finger against the center of my belly and drew the nail down in a line until my belt stopped it.

Ted came in wearing green golf slacks and tasseled loafers without socks and a pale yellow V-necked sweater, and holding a drink.

"You make it to the club?" I said, in some kind of lame offer of friendliness, thinking maybe he'd golfed. He ignored the question and said, "Are you alone?"

I nodded. "He wants her to come home."

"Is she safe there?" Joyce said. "Does he hurt her?"

"Oh," I said, "no. Nothing like that. It's about Donny."

Joyce looked at Ted and said, "We're . . . leaving it up to her for now. If Brigman wants, Ted will talk to him." Ted just stood beside her looking like he'd eaten something rancid.

"She has rules. One is that Donny can only come over if Ted or I is here. If we find out he's been here while we're out, she'll have to go home. You can tell him that."

"He still won't be happy with it."

"Then I guess he'll have to speak to us."

"Can I talk to her?"

"Of course." She turned to go back up the stairs but Chloe was standing there already, watching.

"Come on, Ted," said Joyce.

"Wait," I said, then to Ted, "I'm not here to see Jessi."

"What?"

"You understand," I said, "that this is about Chloe. So, if we could, not have, you know—" I touched my black eye.

He shook his head and made a face and said, "What?"

Joyce's eyes widened slightly as she looked at him, then at me, and said slowly (if one can be said to utter a single word in that way), "Ted?" It seemed to dawn on her then finally what'd been going on. When he looked at her, feigning ignorance, her face flushed and she turned suddenly and stomped away, and he followed.

"So. What?" said Chloe.

"Brigman would like you to come home."

"Well, I'm not."

"He's worried."

"Joyce had the Safe Sex talk with me, if that's what you mean."

"No—I mean, that's good. I'm glad. You should listen to her. But there are things going on, Chloe, some trouble, and you should be there, at home."

"I'm safe here."

"The trouble *is* here."

"Jessi told me."

"No, she didn't."

"Yes, she did."

"Chloe—trust me on this."

"Syd—"

"Listen—"

"I'm staying. Good-bye."

The next morning I took a rear booth where Joyce told me to meet her for breakfast (a quick call to the hospital, a command, a click, no chance to refuse), a nicer place than I usually dined, especially this early.

When she sat down across from me, I said, "So, what'd Ted have to say?"

"About your new friend? Not much. I didn't think he would."

"You didn't know about it before last night?"

"That you were being beaten? You think I'd have let it go on?"

"I don't know."

"Of course you do." She let her fingers play lightly across mine on the table top, then said, "So, how often do you see her?"

"I don't know. Now and then."

"What do you do?"

"Have lunch."

"That's all?"

"More or less."

I should have told her then. And I told myself I would have if she'd asked directly—are you having sex? But she didn't. She said, "I don't understand how having lunch with you has influenced this decision about college."

"I think she's just not sure what she wants to do, and needs some time."

"Is that what she told you?"

"In so many words."

She looked away for several moments and seemed to consider things, then wiped at her eyes and said, "It's going to stop now. Everything. All this violence. You and Jessi. You and Ted. It's over."

"Joyce—"

"I told him, Syd. About us."

I had raised my iced tea to my lips but couldn't swallow.

"About you and me. That that's how it's going to be now."

It was I who wanted to cry then, who saw with a horrible clarity the knot of forces that had been set loose to twist and turn on itself, writhing and furious and self-consuming.

"I'm not sure you understand."

"Syd," she said, "I have a surprise. Come on." She put some cash on the table. We took her car, though she gave me the keys and had me drive. She guided me onto a quiet leafy boulevard of large frame houses in the Old West End and into a driveway, and she led me not into the house but the backyard, to the garage, and up the flight of wooden stairs fastened to the side of it. She produced a new key and unlocked the door at the top.

"For us," she said.

It was a studio apartment outfitted with nothing but two modest though upholstered chairs, a gymnasium-sized bed, and a wooden trunk, which I found held an array of tools and devices and scarves and ropes and oils and unguents and penetrating implements the likes and uses of many of which I had barely imagined let alone used before that.

When she told me to lie down, I did.

*   *   *

Masterson called that afternoon. "I'm sorry, Syd," he said.

"I didn't get it?"

"Well—no."

"Okay."

"The truth is, I never sent in the application. There was a . . . problem. The situation changed."

"I see."

He apologized again and hung up, as if he couldn't bear to hear my voice anymore.

Brigman had several old tire irons in the garage. I took one, angled and tapered at one end for prying off hubcaps with a socket at the other end for fitting over lug nuts, and put it on my passenger seat. So when that night after I turned off the thoroughfare into the neighborhoods behind the med center (I often came this way, traversing a few blocks of ghetto to use the rear entrance, which fed straight into the parking garage) his front grill came up hard on my rear bumper and his big face leered in my mirror, I felt a calmness come over me. And with it the old anger came back. I wondered where it had gone. Though I stopped he pulled around anyway to cut me off.

They were big houses along here, clapboards and shingle-sides and bricks, some duplexes, most with wide front porches where families sat to watch the street, though they didn't stay out at night. The place was dark and dead and I knew that if I were to leap from my car and scream for help, for someone to call the cops, no light would go on, or if it did it would snap off again just as abruptly. The ER got a guy in once who was stabbed right here a block from our entrance and had to drag himself out to the lights of Cherry Street before someone dared to stop and help him.

I rolled down my window and the thick humid air poured in, but he sat looking at me as if (like the animal he was) he smelled a change, sensed that I was done taking his shit. But if he was waiting for me to mosey up so he could nut-grab me again he was kookier than I already thought. He got out so slowly you could practically hear him grunt, as if having to actually work was some big inconvenience. I gripped the iron.

He stood away from my door, a little in front of it, and crouched to look in. He said, "Heya, fuckface. Whyn't you get on out."

I said nothing.

"Come on, otherwise I might have to mess your car up, too."

"Well, there's a threat," I said.

"Listen, I want to talk. I want to know—I mean, you proud, getting the girl to drop out of college? This your big wet dream come true? You like ruining people's lives?"

I said nothing.

"Perfectly happy healthy family, and you gotta come in from your white trash ghetto and fuck it up. Don't look shocked. I know where you live. I watched you and your grease-monkey dad and your freak of a sister. I know what kind of toilet you crawled out of. Thing is, you picked the wrong family. So now you gotta pay."

"What does that mean, Ron?"

"Well, whyn't you tell me? I'd like to know what it's gonna take with you. But we'll figure it out."

"Fuck you."

"Yeah? Get out." Then he made his mistake. He stepped up to my door and pulled the handle, which was locked, so he raised his left hand to the sill and lifted the lock. I swung the iron across in front of me, wrist-slapped with it really, because there was of course no room to take a good swing, but it was one of those unconscious physical things that sometimes work because you haven't planned it to death, you just react and let the old eye-hand work its magic. It put a nice dent in my door, so you can imagine what it did to him. He howled and leapt, his bulk coming straight up off the ground, and spun while he was airborne in a kind of grotesque pirouette, and then danced, swearing, moaning, gurgling in his throat, hands pressed between his fire-hydrant thighs.

This was when I made my own mistake—instead of pulling it into gear and taking off, I watched him (fascinated frankly and a little stunned at what I'd done), so I was unprepared for his sudden recovery. All in a motion, as he leapt in pain and fury, spinning like a cartoon, he spun right back to my door and yanked the handle, which this time worked, and then reached in and grabbed my shirt and dragged me out so that I found myself on the graveled asphalt.

I struggled up, frantic to get to my feet before he could plant a boot in my face, and had just made it when in his spinning and howling he drove his fat head into my chest and knocked me so hard into the car that my own head snapped back and I went down again and didn't move this time. I was conscious but only marginally (much of this I reconstructed later). I dimly remember lying with my head under my car. It was still running; I smelled exhaust. And I remember him kicking me, as I knew he would.

I don't know how long I lay there. I knew I had broken bones. When I was able to sit up, blood ran into my face, and I felt it running down under my collar as well. I managed to crawl back into my car and drive somehow, hanging on the wheel, wiping my eyes to find my way in through the rear gate of the compound and around the great building itself to the entrance of the ER. Then I seemed to be sliding down some slope, though I was aware enough to remember resting my bloody pounding face on the pad in the center of the steering wheel and the horn going off as I slipped away.

SIXTEEN

I retain dim fragments of images from that night—Phyllis and Ray alternately leaning over me, Brigman showing up frantic and frightened. And strangely, Ted. I remember seeing him with Phyllis at one point in the walkway outside the curtained stall, and later in the room with me, though I was to wonder eventually whether it was a vision, an illusion, a dream perhaps, for even as I saw it I slid away down the slope again.

When I woke finally and knew where I was (though I wasn't sure why yet) I turned my head, painful as that was, and saw Brigman dozing in a chair. Beyond him someone walked past in the dimly lighted hallway. He stirred then and said, "Heya."

We regarded one another.

"You remember what happened?"

"I don't know," I said.

"You got your clock cleaned." I had, he told me, a concussion, twenty-five stitches in my head, a broken wrist, and several cracked ribs. He added, "They think you got mugged." He let that sit a moment, then said, "You understand anything?"

"Starting to."

"I mean, are you really awake now? You feel groggy?"

I was, still, but I said, "I'm pretty clear."

"They been worried about you sleeping." He slid his chair closer to my bed and said, "So was it him?"

"Yeah. I think I broke his hand."

"You should'a broke his fuckin neck."

"Next time."

"Fuck that." He got up and went over to the window. Dawn was turning, the sky just cracking with first light. "There ain't gonna be a next time." He pulled out a cigarette and put it in his mouth but didn't light it. He said, "You gotta stop it. Clean up your mess. And we gotta get Chloe. Then we'll take care of this motherfucker." It occurred to me to ask which motherfucker he was talking about, Ted or Ron, but I didn't. I just let it float there between us.

He sat with me until I dozed again. When I woke into the full morning he was gone. They came in to take a temp and b.p. and shine a light in my eyes and when they went out someone else came in. I must have started because he, Ted, said, "Shh. Just relax."

"What are you doing here?"

"We need to talk."

"No, we don't. It's past that now. You don't know what you're in for."

"Syd—" He shook his head. "I'm frightened."

"You should be. I can sue your ass off."

"Will you shut up? If you weren't so full of . . ." He held up his hand and said, "I'm sorry. I'm sorry. But you're missing my point. You can't hurt me in that way. You don't have anything. Call a lawyer. Call the FBI if you want. I don't care, except for one thing, the thing you've always known would scare me—"

"I'm not going to hurt her."

"Really? Do you think she has any idea what's going on?"

"No, of course not."

"And if she finds out? She's changed her life because of you. I don't know if you realize what you've done to her—"

"She just needs time to think—"

"Oh, bullshit. She's in love with you. She thinks you love her."

"I never meant her to."

"What you meant hardly matters at this point."

Of course he was right. He surely wasn't telling me anything I hadn't known since that July Fourth afternoon when Joyce squeezed me in the pool and I knew what was going to happen, knew that I could never say no to her, could never not go back.

"Her welfare is my only concern now," he said. "The rest is just history. I don't know how you really feel about her. I don't know if you even know. But if you care anything for her, outside of whatever else has happened, how you feel about me or Joyce, then you should be frightened, too."

"I am."

"Then do something about it. Stop this nonsense with Joyce. Not because of me—because frankly I don't care anymore—but because of her."

I could only nod.

"You've won," he said. "You got me back. But now it's time to stop. Then, when the time comes, I'll help you."

"Like you did with that fellowship?"

"What do you mean? I wrote the letter."

"Must've been great. Masterson didn't even submit the application."

He looked at me for a moment, then smiled and shook his head. "You have no idea what you've got yourself into."

"What do you mean?"

"I wrote a perfectly good letter, Syd."

"Then what happened?"

"Who wants you to stay here? Who's manipulative and selfish and crazy enough to make sure you do?"

"She called Masterson?"

"I'd guess she called Dotty. Little chat, you know. And said just enough that Dotty had to tell Dave. Enough that he'd smell the stink and drop you."

"I can't believe that."

"Ask yourself something—who was it on those videotapes, be-ing watched? Who was the focus of all that? Who can turn her emotions on and off like hot water to make them whatever the sit-uation demands? Who craves going to bars to be hit on while at the same time being watched? Whose idea was that? Who *begged* me to be allowed to play, to be seen in that way?"

"That's a lie. She said—"

"What? What've I ever done, Syd, besides fulfill her desires, by watching or whatever, and then to be there for her, with her, after? And for that matter, what have *you* ever done but the same thing?"

I felt dizzy and nauseous.

He said, "I know what people say about me, even in my own house. Jessi calls me a narcissist. On some level it's become a fam-ily joke. Ha ha, Daddy's looking in the mirror again. And I'm the first to admit that I have an ego. But I'm not dysfunctional. There's a mental illness called narcissistic personality disorder. *I* don't have that. I'm not sick. I'm just a guy who likes to succeed, and keep his hair trimmed. And I like running a big lab and hav-ing influence and making money and driving a nice car. Is that horrid? You're no different. And neither of us is by any measure pathological."

"And she is?"

He didn't answer that. He said, "Rest, now. It's not too late. Are they discharging you?"

"I think so."

"Take whatever sick time you need." He touched me just briefly on the shoulder and turned to leave and nearly ran into Brigman. I saw Brigman's eyes flick to the hook and back up, and braced for whatever threat or profanity was going to come out of his mouth, but he said nothing. And strangely (because he was looking not at me when he said it but at Brigman) Ted said, "Thank you," and brushed past him and went out.

Later when I saw how we were getting home—Donny was

waiting under the portico in his Road Runner—I knew what it meant. And when, a few hours after he'd dropped us off, he showed up again, this time with Chloe and her suitcases, and after that took my car (which he and Brigman had picked up from the police lot where it'd been towed) across to his side of the street and began pounding out the ruined sheet metal, it merely confirmed it. The forces had been marshaled. Rifts had been, if not healed, then patched over. Chloe was to be given some autonomy, which meant that what she did with Donny was her business. In return for that, what Brigman would get was the most unquestioningly loyal muscle-bound muscle-headed mechanically gifted minion a marine going into battle could ask for.

Though I slept through the afternoon it felt even then as if I were waiting. Toward evening Jessi came. It had been arranged. Brigman and Chloe both had to work. She sat with me on a dining room chair someone had carried up until it was dark out, until Chloe came home and I listened to them downstairs chattering and laughing together until I drifted off again.

The next day I could feel the effects of the concussion ameliorating, a fading of fogginess as my mind brightened and the world came into focus again. I walked over to look at my car. Donny had already made huge progress. He'd picked up a whole new door at a junkyard, and pounded the fender out so it was ready to be Bondo'd and sanded back to its original smoothness. He said he could fix the crease in the driver's door, too, where I'd broken Ron's hand. After that, all he had left was the painting, and that was his finest talent. As I turned to leave, he said, "I never done nothing with her. Not even now."

"What?"

"If you think I would, you're an asshole."

I stood for a moment and looked at him, then walked down to the thoroughfare at the end of the block, and around to the next street and was just coming back when the yellow Rabbit slowed

beside me and Ron leaned across and looked out his open passenger window. I may have yelled. I don't remember. He didn't say
anything. Just reached across and flipped me the bird with his left
hand. He couldn't use the right one for that purpose, since it was
casted from fingertips to mid-forearm. Then he pointed at me, as
if to say I was marked, and drove off.

Later, when I told Brigman, he didn't respond except to set his
jaw and nod a little.

I called my professors and explained what had happened, and
figured out what I'd missed. Finals were barely two weeks away.

I rested another day. Then the following morning, which dawned
overcast and wet and looked as if it would stay that way, Jessi
drove me to school. Later Chloe got me before she had to go to
work. That afternoon, Donny came over to say it was ready. He'd
painted the whole thing, replaced the drab army gray-greenness
with a deeper more verdant autumnal shade. I thanked him several times and asked what I owed him. (I'd filed a police report after Jessi gave me the license number. A few days later an insurance
agent called, asked a few questions, then mumbled something
about how I wasn't the first victim of this guy but I was sure going
to be the last that that company covered. A week later I got a
check for nearly eight hundred dollars.) He said Brigman'd taken
care of it. I was okay to drive by then, steering with the casted
hand and shifting with the good. So I took it around the block at
first, then farther out into the city.

I thought I was just driving, seeing how it felt, but I ended up
somehow on the block of Scottwood where Joyce had rented her
little pad and drove past and saw that her car was not there. I
wasn't sure why I was doing this. Would I have stopped if I'd seen
the 280Z? I didn't know. But now, sure that she wasn't there, I did
stop. I wanted to leave her a note. I tore out a piece of notebook
paper and climbed the wetted steps to leave it in the storm door. It
was going to say something profound and considered like "I'm all

right. Let's talk. Syd." But it didn't get written because as I reached the top of the staircase, Joyce opened the door.

"Oh," I said. "I didn't see your car."

"It's in the alley in back." She was barefooted, and though it was oddly chilly for an August day, even a rainy one, she wore only a bright yellow sun dress.

"I'm sorry—"

"Would you like to come in?"

"Is it all right?"

"Why wouldn't it be?"

"Have you talked to Ted?"

"About what?"

"Everything."

"I know what's going on, Syd, if that's what you mean."

I went in after her. She closed the door behind us, and I put my hand on her arm because I needed to touch her and she smiled, and said, "You look like hell."

"Thank you."

"I don't just mean the injuries. You're greasy."

"Yeah, well, it's kind of hard to wash."

"It hurts?"

"Plus with only one hand."

"It just takes practice."

I sat in one of the easy chairs while she went back to the kitchenette where she'd apparently been cleaning.

"How come you're here?" I asked.

"I'm pretty much living here."

"Really? God. Joyce—"

"I'm happy, Syd. I just—I get lonely. Listen—how would you like me to wash your head?"

"Really?"

"I won't hurt you. Much."

I took my shirt off and went to the sink and leaned into it and was struck not only by a pulsing (though not exactly pain) in the contusions themselves but a deeper thrumming inside the cranium that after a moment segued to a staggering vertigo. I had to kneel with my hands on the edge of the basin and close my eyes.

She said, "Are you okay in the shower?"

"Yeah."

"Then we'll do that."

How she meant, I wasn't sure. She pulled the last few slices from a plastic bread bag and shook the crumbs in the sink and slid it over my cast and taped it. It was an old-looking bathroom, from the thirties I figured, done in pink and black tiles and heavy porcelain fixtures, the freestanding tub high and claw-footed with a double curtain that went all the way around it on a wire, and a retrofitted showerhead connected to the faucet via rubber tubing. After I got under it, I heard the door open and close.

"Are you all right?"

"Yes."

"Let's try this." She separated the curtains and reached in and I sort of squatted while she squeezed on the shampoo and tried to work it in, but it was a reach for her—I was taller anyway and the old tub increased that difference by another five inches—and she was getting pretty wet. She said, "Hang on."

I stood with my eyes closed and waited. The curtains separated again and she said, "Move over," and got in with me. I reached out and my hand found her breast.

"Turn around," she said, and began to knead my stitched and greasy head and rarely in my life I think have I felt anything so satisfying and competent. She washed even the sutured areas, and scraped the rest of it with her nails so that the scalp itself burned and came alive again. She said, "Nice?"

"Yeah. It hurts a little, but it's nice."

"Isn't that always the way?"

She helped me rinse, then began to scrub the rest of me using her nails on the dry skin, washed my chest and back and belly and then soaped down over my ass and between my legs and reached around front as if it were just a normal part of washing a body and began to move her hand back and forth on the erection she found there. I came almost immediately. And then she started to get out.

When I fitted my good hand between her legs, so that it covered her, she shook her head, but lifted one foot to the edge of the tub and steadied herself against me. She came nearly as quickly as I had. By the time I'd rinsed and opened the curtains she'd pulled the dress over her head. She opened the door and went out.

I took down a towel and put my face into it when I heard Joyce say, "Oh!" as if Fear itself had been waiting for her. I stepped out of the tub and, thinking she'd slipped, maybe, or hurt herself some other way, opened the door. The outside doorway was open and Jessi stood in it, heavy gray daylight seeping in around her so that I could not really make out her expression. But I heard her say, "Oh. Oh— what is this? What is it? Syd?" She sounded as if she were shivering.

I hugged the towel. I shivered, too, cold with the fresh air. It was my name she said, only mine, and it must have been me she was looking at, not her mother, so it was for me to speak, for me to answer, but I did not. Joyce said, "Sweetie, Syd was having trouble. With his wounds. He asked me for some help."

"Is that true?"

I nodded. I said, "The stitches didn't feel right. I didn't know if I could take a shower."

"So you had to come here to do it?"

"She just looked, to see if there was a problem, then made me take a shower because I was gross."

"Honey," Joyce said, "I was just checking on him. I'm sorry if you think it looks funny. You startled me."

"But you knew I was coming over."

"I—I just wasn't thinking about it. I mean, I didn't think—I was just surprised to see someone standing there."

I understood what we were then, Joyce and I, and that I would always look at her. Whatever else it was, if she wanted someone to look, I would look. Her husband was finished looking. Now her daughter was looking, though that would not happen again. But I would always look.

Jessi spoke again, to me. "That book," she said.

"What?"

"That fucking Aristotle. She never wanted to see that. You never even talked to her about it, did you? It's so stupid."

"Jessi, come on."

"No. I didn't get it then. I mean, I got it—I knew you'd come to see her, she was why you were there. The book was just an excuse for my benefit. But I didn't know why you wanted to see her. I thought you were just her friend. I'm so stupid."

"Why are you talking about this? What difference does it make now?"

"Because I knew," she said, "or I should have."

"Jessi—"

But she had turned and gone.

"Baby," Joyce said, and some remaining shred of maternal instinct overwhelmed her, at least for that moment. She said, "My god," and she left, too, in her yellow dress and bare feet, plucked her keys from the hook on the wall by the door and ran down the staircase into the rain.

SEVENTEEN

I thought about going over, even yearned (a part of me at least) to go, but it came clear as I lay in my room that I had no place at that house anymore. I'd somehow suddenly become irrelevant to their lives. I stared out the window. Though we still had the sun of summer it was weakened on that late afternoon, aging and preparing its fade into the paler flatter briefer sunlight of autumn. Eventually, I fell asleep.

When I opened my eyes it took me a moment to realize in the inky dark that I was not alone, that there was a face hovering directly over mine, peering down at me. I flinched.

"It'll be over now," Brigman said. You could smell that he'd been drinking.

"What will?"

He looked at me.

"You mean Ron?"

He almost nodded.

"It doesn't matter anymore. Jessi. I've got to—what are you talking about? What're you going to do?"

"Did. You hungry? I brought some dinner."

"What'd you do?"

"It don't concern you no more."

"How do you figure that?"

"Come on," he said, "let's eat."

"How the fuck do you figure that?" I shouted after him.

It was some excuse for Mexican he'd picked up, soggy of tortilla and dry of bean and meat, but I was hungry and so was he apparently because we tucked in and made not a sound except the grinding salivating noises of hard male mastication. We'd just finished and sat back, him to smoke, me to sip one of the Cokes he'd bought, when the front door slammed open and heavy feet stomped in and back toward the kitchen—Chloe's as it turned out. She stalked over to me, put her face down in mine and said, "What'd you do?"

"What?"

"She came to my work. She was standing in the middle of the stupid mall, *screaming*."

"Where is she?"

"What'd you *do*?"

"Never mind that, Chloe. Where is she?"

"I don't *know*. I took her in the back—which I am really not allowed to do, I would get fired if they found out—and she sat there sobbing, and then I had customers, and when I came back she'd gone out through the loading dock door. What the hell?"

I shook my head.

"Syd!"

"I don't know."

She looked at Brigman and said, "What do you know?"

He drew on his smoke and looked at her. The Buddha of Beer. When he finally shrugged, she exhaled in exasperation.

"Listen," I said, "can I talk to her?"

"I don't know where she is! Why would you think she wants to talk to you, anyway?"

"She doesn't, I'm sure. But someone needs to find her."

"Well, you should have thought about that," she said, as I got up to leave. "Before you did whatever stupid thing you did."

*   *   *

Ted was alone at the house. He stood aside and let me in and did not to my surprise criticize me or even give so much as a slight shake of the head or tightening of the lips in regret or chastisement. He simply said, "Hello, Syd."

"I'd like to talk to her," I said. "I think I can make it better. I think I can explain."

"You can't," he said, "but she's not here, anyway. I don't know where she is. I'm frightened. If you can find her . . ."

"Joyce—"

"She's not here, either."

"Today—Joyce went after her."

"I know. I saw her this afternoon. Joyce. She was here."

I stepped back to leave, there being nothing else really to say, when he said, "She left you something." He took an envelope from his dressing gown pocket.

"Why?"

"Read it," he said.

"My dear Syd," it said. "I think that we must not see each other after this, not even for a moment, at least not for some time. I am leaving. I must, I feel. I've discussed this with my husband and he feels strongly that it's the right thing to do, to begin to let things heal to whatever extent they can, and more important, not to make them worse. So I'm going away, tonight. I will not talk to you for some time. Maybe, one day, we can see each other again. Yours, Joyce."

"How can she just leave?" I said.

"She just can. It's best, don't you think?"

"No. This—" I waved the note. I was furious. She'd signed it "yours," for god's sake. Not even love. What did that mean? It was as stupid and insipid as it could be.

He nodded. "You see now why it's necessary? You're upset, in spite of everything. You can't let her go."

"I can—"

"No," he said, "you can't. And you wouldn't. You didn't. You haven't, at a great cost to us all. So she has finally seen what was necessary, and to her credit she's done it."

"She *left*?"

"She hasn't abandoned anyone. She'll come back. But by then things will have cooled."

I shook my head.

"The thing now," he said, "is to find Jessi. It's urgent, Syd."

"Is he out looking?"

"Who?"

"Ron."

He looked at me. He said, "Who?"

"The guy—"

"Who did that to you?"

"Yeah. You hired him."

"I had someone follow you when I wasn't sure what was going on. In June. But not since then. I don't know this guy."

I understood then who'd been paying him to have me beaten until I quit with Jessi.

I burned through most of a tank and filled up sometime around midnight but she was nowhere I knew to look, none of the places we'd gone together. I went by Joyce's apartment as well, a couple of times, actually, and sat in my car in the street watching it for any sign of life. I even went up once but the door was locked.

Our house was dark, too, when I got home. I turned on the tube and had a beer, thinking it would help me sleep, but I'd slept all evening and my body was ready to go to work. I was going to be tortured I could tell by a night of sitting with nothing to do but fret. I waited through *The Tomorrow Show* with Tom Snyder, then crept upstairs wanting at least to rest my eyes and I did slip into a shallow doze. When I awoke my clock said four A.M. I lay listening, wondering, and then heard again what it was that had roused me—Brigman's alarm.

A joke—that's what I thought at first, or rather told myself. But when I heard him drag himself up, throw some water in his face, and more than that when I heard him open the door downstairs to let someone in, and listened until I heard that the other voice was Donny's, I knew it was no joke. And when from Brigman's bedroom window I watched the two of them toss shovels into the back of the blue electrician's truck they'd borrowed somewhere and climb into the cab, such a surge of urgency flooded through me that I felt crazed, crazy. I was already dressed. I raced downstairs, grabbed a jacket, got in my car and tore off after them. It was an old slow truck and it was nothing to find them and follow. The trick was in not coming up too tight behind so they could see me. I turned in fact and went around entire blocks so as to seem like another random car—and when they got to the Trail and headed downtown it was easy then to fit in with the thin traffic.

We followed exactly the route I drove when I took Brigman over on that early spring morning to look at the 'Cuda, exactly until we came down the far side of the High Level Bridge, where they turned off onto Miami Street, which ran south along the river. I went past it, cut down a side street, raced along and even blew some stop signs until I could turn and park and kill my lights just as they crawled past me. In that way I watched them and could just make it out as they, too, turned into the parking lot of a boarded-up carryout with a Budweiser sign still on the front, and stopped. They were waiting for there to be no traffic, I figured, and sure enough as soon as the road appeared deserted they crept out and across to where there were no other roads or houses or anything but trees and then the embankment leading down to the river itself, and they seemed to poke along there for a moment until they found what they were looking for and turned into the trees. I watched their headlights work back along some dirt turnoff that'd been carved out in the foliage until Donny killed the engine.

It was three blocks from where I'd parked. I ran up the road, crossed over, and crept into the trees until I was close enough to hear them pulling things out of the truck, the shovels, yes, I heard scraping, but other things, too, heavier sounding things, though I dared not move closer to see. They made a couple trips. After the last one I waited a good fifteen minutes before creeping through to the truck. It was parked at the head of a faint footpath which, quietly as I could, moving a step (pausing), then another, I followed down.

Picture an omnipresent grayness. I imagine it now as a fine ash coating everything with a simultaneous fog permeating the non-corporeal (spirits, thoughts, ambitions, moods). The great gray river, frigid and foamy and dirty and deep, formed the backdrop. We were perched at its edge, in the very gut of the city but in one of those lost spots that exist between the meaningful places of commerce and transport and education and life.

When I came down the pathway of course it was still dark, and darker still in that empty barren place. I could hear them, though—they were digging. I crawled up the face of a slaggy heap of limestone, to the top so I could see over when it lightened. The stone itself lay at the base of the higher slope and as it did finally begin to lighten, after what felt like an hour of listening to them work, I could see that it was covered in gray brown grass that ought, I thought, to have been ashamed of itself. From where I sat hidden I could hear the hum and swoosh of the early morning traffic but it couldn't see me, or any of us. If I'd put my arm out to ten o'clock, it would've pointed at a railroad trestle over the river. At eleven the trestle ended at the huge (gray) concrete tubes of a storage elevator. Next to these towers, directly across, was a warehouse with the faded word "Warehouse" painted on its side. Up-river lay the High Level Bridge and then the downtown. But no one over there could see us. The slope continued in both directions and was covered in careless brush, saplings and bushes and vines and weeds, all gray, all accidental, that closed us in, hid us from the world.

At the base of the heap of stone—I began to see with the sunrise—lay an open area marked only by more pathetic grass and cracked up slabs of faded asphalt and two huge cleats where the cargo ships tied on when they were backed up in line from the various elevators and cranes and warehouses lining the river from the lake clear through the city and on to the southern industrial townlets that existed, like the rest of it, for a single two-headed purpose—to absorb raw material from the river that fed it, and then to excrete back what it had made.

Digging they were, indeed. And drinking already at this earliest hour. I could just make it out as Donny paused, panting, wiped his brow, then drained the beer Brigman handed him and threw the empty in the dark hole. He squatted then and blew for a minute until Brigman said something and they started in to dig again.

At first, I could only sit shivering in the damp dark, huddled into the rock and curled into myself. I found that if I stayed like that a kind of warmth came. I'd heard you felt warm as you froze to death and remember thinking how wonderful it was of the world to make such a rule. I thought about what Jessi'd said once about drowning, how it was wonderful, too, a thing that maybe made you feel dimly, at the bare edges of your dying consciousness, regret that you could only experience this spectacle once.

Then, as I became aware of the first real light, I sat up a little and peered over and a shock ran through me as I saw it for the first time—Brigman and Donny were standing up to their shoulders in a hole that was maybe six feet long and a couple wide. Though they were some distance back from the river, and well higher than its surface, gray water had risen to their knees. If I was cold they must have been numb except for the exertion that kept them going, them reaching down in and throwing out mud.

It was misting out, getting ready to rain, so we would all soon be wet one way or the other. My legs ached. Walking sounded wonderful. But they kept on lifting sopping bladefuls of mud and water from the hole.

It was really only then—as if I had been in some kind of trance before that, some dream I refused to wake from—that I finally un-

derstood (though I had known it already in the heart of my heart)
how far it had gone, how far I had taken it, what calamity I had
wrought. And to what length this beaten and worn man would
go, had gone already, for me and for the dream that had come to
belong to him. I should have wept at that insight. I should have
run crying down that hill and hugged him, and Donny, too, for his
simple blind loyalty. But they would have just pushed me off and
swore and spit, and dug some more.

They didn't go much farther before Brigman threw his shovel
onto the ground and climbed out. It was coming on real daylight
now and they would soon risk being seen. Donny stopped, too,
but did not climb out yet. He stood looking at what he had
wrought.

And as he did, Brigman, in a strange and furtive movement, slid
around behind him. I tried to sit up straighter but slipped in the
loose stone. Brigman raised his shovel, aimed its pointed blade at
that spot where Donny's neck joined his skull. He pulled back, as
if he were cocking a gun. God, I saw it all then. All my notions of
revenge and rectification were insipid little boy tantrums next to
this, this genius of evil, this end of all ends. I'd been wrong. This
was not about me and my iniquities after all. And a part of me
hoped wildly that that was so, that I might let go of the dread I'd
been carrying around, though I knew it would only be replaced
with a different dread. The hole was dug now. It would be filled
one way or the other.

I felt my fingertips. I felt the damp air playing across my face
and found that I could suddenly smell the river again and the dirt
and rock and the dampness in the air.

Brigman stepped forward and began to thrust.

"No!" I shouted. It was a tiny sound there on that stone hill, in
the brush and mud and all the other detritus of the city. It went
out over the river and died.

But even in mid-shout it came to me that Brigman was probably just screwing around, fantasizing what he might have done in
a different world. He looked up at me, at where I sat. Both of

them did. Then I heard Brigman say, "Shit." I knew the expression on his face, though I couldn't quite see it—the tightening of the corners of his mouth into that smirk I'd evoked in him on a fairly regular basis over the years of my later childhood and youth.

It changed nothing, their knowledge of my presence there—it couldn't at that point. They had to finish. Donny crawled out and then the two of them walked a few paces to some high grass, to something bound there that I had not noticed before—a long something bound in greenish-gray moving quilts and rings of silver duct tape. It was a body, of course, the body they'd been digging the grave for. The body of Ron, whom Brigman had somehow—whether in murderous rage or frigid calculation—rendered threatless forevermore. They carried it between them to the hole. It was no ceremony, I can tell you. They dumped it in and with barely another glance at it began quickly to fill in their work, though not before I could see it in there, the head and the knees sort of floating until the dirt pushed it down.

I turned away and leaned forward and vomited between my legs. I don't know how much time passed but when I looked over again the hole was gone. Brigman and Donny tamped the dirt with the backs of their shovels, and the smacking sound spread up into the mist.

After they covered the wound in the earth with brush I stood and headed down, my feet sliding in the slag so that as I and the small avalanche I created reached the bottom, the two of them were just coming past. I fell into file behind Donny. As we marched up the narrow muddy path to the road where the borrowed truck was concealed, the skies opened and it began to pour.

It was only then, from the top of the slope, from the copse of trees near the roadside, that we saw the red flashing lights of emergency vehicles tearing up toward the apex of the bridge—cops, I figured, of course coming to get us. We could see them clearly from where we stood, though it was actually quite some distance away. I felt resigned to it almost, that it would end this way in ignominious disgrace and a lifetime of nothing to look forward to ever again. But they stopped, these two vehicles, right there at the top, at the very highest point on the bridge—at precisely the spot where Jessi and I had parked that once to look over.

And then I knew. I cried out and Brigman in his intuition of me seemed to know, too, because he just said, "Get in," and I did. I squeezed into the center of the seat, the stick shift between my legs, and Donny backed up and turned around, and they sat for just a moment in the trees, waiting for a break in the traffic in case someone should see them and remember the truck (though in that darkness and driving rain I don't know who would have been paying any attention—they couldn't have planned it better) and then pulled out and raced toward the eastern foot of the bridge. When we got there it was closed off already, a squad car blocking the way, the cop in the driver's seat with his window partially opened and him sipping coffee.

Donny stopped. I told Brigman to get out, and I ran through the rain up along the line of commuting cars toward the sidewalk that followed the roadway to the bridge's crest.

"Hey!" the cop shouted out his window, and got out.

"I know her," I yelled, pointing.

"What?" He wore a green plastic poncho over his uniform.

"It's a girl, right?"

He just looked at me, then pulled his radio from his belt.

"I have to go," I said.

"Stop it!" he said. "Get back!"

But I was running again and it was just him alone, so he couldn't abandon his post, and probably he was relieved about that anyway because he didn't have to get too soaked. He must have radioed but they were too busy then, the rescue workers and the cops at the top, trying to talk her down, to bother with me.

And I wonder sometimes what would have happened if I hadn't

gone up, if it would have turned out differently. She was the kind of girl who, having made up her mind, did not wonder much after that.

When I got close enough I could see that it was her, Jessi, and how she stood outside of the railing, reaching back behind so that she could hold on and lean forward, out over the sheer drop to the river. A cop crouched on the sidewalk, speaking to her and holding out a hand as if it would calm her. And up the river then, through the curtains of rain, I saw more flashing lights, these on the water, a boat of some kind, Coast Guard or city police, making its way toward us.

So I could see her and the whole situation laid out there before me, and that was when I called out her name. I don't know if she heard it and stopped to look, or rather if she just looked one last time to see if anything about the world had suddenly changed. But her eyes locked on mine in that moment, and we froze and regarded each other in the instant that would come to define whatever was left of both our lives. Afterward the cops said nothing about it, did not chastise or criticize me for anything. They simply asked questions—who I was, how I knew her.

But in that moment of the boat racing and the cop talking and me staring and the sun trying to rise through the rain clouds and the summer of that year of 1979 ending and our city awakening and stretching out in its tired sodden beauty beneath us, Jessi seemed to straighten herself, to stand taller for a moment, to pull herself back toward the railing and look out and away, down the river toward the docks and the elevators and toward the answer to a question that would now never be answered: what was it like, that moment of drowning? Then she turned around, faced us, climbed over the railing, and came to me without looking at anyone else there. Came to me and into my arms, and collapsed.

EIGHTEEN

She was admitted that morning to the psych unit at St. V's and so of course I couldn't see her then. After she got out, though (and began what became years of counseling), I did. I don't know if it was because of my presence there on the bridge when she came down, or even if I was the reason she came down, but somehow she did not recoil in horror at my face when I came over after she returned home. What drove her to the brink of her death was not discussed by us on that day, or on any day since. It became The Thing That Never Happened. The event itself, the near leap, the cry for help, became simply The Accident.

What happened then was that I couldn't leave her. Whether it was due to guilt or a sense of responsibility or perhaps the affection I had begun to feel for her, in the aftermath, I kept coming around long after simple decency would have allowed me to stop. Sometimes we just sat and read for hours, neither of us feeling the need to speak.

What allowed this to continue (both my visiting and our never referring to what had happened) was the fact that Joyce did not return. Months passed. I continued to go over nearly every day, and still Joyce didn't come. As it turned out, she never would. Whatever life she went off to, whatever loves and family she was to find, remained a mystery.

I like to imagine that she knew her presence there would be destructive. She'd said as much in that last note. Still, I confess that I waited for her and did not know what would happen if she showed up. No, that is wrong—I knew. And so did she, I think, and for that reason as much as any other she gave up the chance of seeing her daughter again. I have not communicated with her at all, in any way, though Ted, the few times I asked him about it, long ago, intimated that he had some idea of where she was. Anyway, far too much river finally passed beneath that great bridge for it to matter anymore.

Jessi started that January after The Accident at the U, and in two and a half years earned an honors B.S. in Biology. I finally graduated, too, a year after she started, and smoked the MCATs, but I went to work as a bench tech in Ted's lab. (I actually took Ray's spot in Chemistry. He finally had a blowout with Ted that led either to his quitting or getting fired, depending on who you asked, but it was a good thing for him. He went into sales for a laboratory supply company and grew fat and rich.)

In the summer of 1982 Jessi resurrected an old desire, a thing we'd discussed once a long time before, and talked me into accompanying her on a European bum around. And in a small walkup pension almost next door to the Sorbonne sometime on a July afternoon after we'd eaten a nice park-bench lunch of bread and a cheese called L'Edel de Claron and fresh pears and a bottle of Pouilly-Fuissé, and then taken a nap, we made love for the first time since The Accident. (I mean, not only to each other, but to anyone—I had remained as chaste as she had. I don't know why. It wasn't some noble decision I made or anything. It started that way and then stuck.) We were in France a month, then spent two weeks whipping through Germany and Italy, and a few days in Amsterdam before flying home—not exactly long enough to call it bumming around but enough for a decent look. In addition to satisfying her dream, and allowing finally the re-consummation of our relationship, the trip also served the purpose of steeling us against the grind we were both to begin that fall.

She'd decided after she graduated to apply to med school. She insisted I apply, too. Case accepted us both. I could have qualified for aid and was prepared to take out a pile of loans but Ted floored me by offering to pay my way. The whole nut.

So when we got home we moved together into an apartment off Deering Avenue on Cleveland's East Side. Jessi was twenty-two; I was twenty-seven. In the summer of the following year we were married. Three years after that we became doctors.

The summer Chloe graduated from high school she married Donny. A few years later she helped him open a body shop and over time he came to be locally famous for his high-end paint jobs. Chloe took some business classes at the U and they opened a second shop, and eventually a third. They live now with their two kids in a big old house in one of the posh little settlements well downriver from the city, where their backyard rolls down a great emerald hill right to the water and they have a huge dock and a couple of boats. Ted and old Masterson, it turned out, had been discussing Chloe's face from the time they met her. Neither had ever seen a facial nevus flammeus quite that severe, and eventually they hooked her up with a top plastics man in Cincinnati. The first steps, which were a surgery and then sessions with a dermatologic makeup consultant, greatly ameliorated the stain. Eventually with laser surgeries and everything that was to come, the mark, even without makeup, has greatly faded, leaving more the impression of an uneven tan rather than a stain. The funny thing is that I don't think Donny ever really cared how it looked, anyway. I knew, by the way, that day when he told me he'd never touched Chloe, that he was telling the truth. He was never someone who knew how to lie. So for that, and the fact that he was there for me when my life was at its darkest and most desperate, and mostly his acceptance of my sister's face for what it was and his lack of any sort of judgment about it, his blindness to it—he earned and will forever have my deepest gratitude.

Jessi and I did our first three years of residency at the Cleveland Clinic, where we began our respective specialties, I in pathology and Jessi in psychiatry. Then she earned a fellowship in Ann Arbor. I was able to hook up (again through some intervention of Ted's) with the Detroit Receiving Hospital and then the very busy Wayne County Coroner's Office, and so we moved north to the suburban haven of Livonia from which we commuted in opposite directions. We were there another three years and thought for a time that we might stay in the area but in the end came to see where we belonged and so moved home. Jessi initially joined a group and went into private practice but it wasn't long before she broke away to found an institute, ultimately a hugely successful one complete with its own campus and a large staff and even a residential facility for in-patients and research as well, all of which she directs. She is only forty-three as of this writing, and has a long career still ahead of her. The money she makes is breathtaking. I tell people that my salary just about pays the taxes on what she brings in, though that is a slight exaggeration of my earnings.

I apologize if I'm rushing this. It is all a continuum to me, though, the gradual evolution of our lives, and seems startling only in the rare moments when I am able to look back upon it as a whole. But each day we wake up and go off into the world and do our jobs and come home at the end like everyone else, and there's nothing after all very startling about that. Except, of course, that there is.

PART FIVE

If the goal is having some space in which to live one's own life, then it is desirable that the account of specific injustices dissolve into a more general understanding that human beings everywhere do terrible things to one another.

—SUSAN SONTAG,
Regarding the Pain of Others (2003)

NINETEEN

When I stand, my knees are so stiff I can hardly straighten them. Age comes, I guess, in this way. I look up around me and it is as if the lights and the crowd have just suddenly appeared, as if I am in the pit of an amphitheater, at the center of the action, of attention, a kind of celebrity suddenly, when just moments before it was only me hiding on a pile of cold stone.

This place is no longer a wasteland, or rather it will not be much longer. In the fullness of time, as they say, the city fathers (who were once nearly all blue-collar populists but are now, in the new way of the world, largely business-friendly moralizers) real-ized the immense value of the riverfront, any riverfront within sight of the downtown, and have issued licenses and permits and contracts so that it will soon all be developed. This particular spot (which still for the time being looks across at a warehouse that says " a ehou e" on its side) is going to be condominiums. The contractor's men who have been preparing the ground to accept the huge pilings that will hold the buildings up away from the riverbank and the gray river itself when it swells and rises have been digging, of course, and in the process of that digging uncov-ered the apparent crown of a skull, an especially round and hominoidish-looking one.

The foreman was at first merely angry and impatient, hoping still it was just the top of the head of a large dog or something but, in good conscience and remiss as he was to delay the work, called the authorities to have someone come down and take a look. Who came was a homicide detective I know pretty well, a man named Dennis Lewandowski, who knows his business and was pretty sure when he stood in the deep cut of earth and looked at this white orb sticking out, and pushed his fingers a little further into the dirt and revealed the high forehead and the huge forward-facing eye sockets, that it was the head of an actual human being. Needless to say construction stopped and I was immediately notified.

I am and have been for some years now the deputy coroner and associate medical examiner for Lucas County, this county in which I grew up, so I'm pretty well versed in just such things as human remains that happen to turn up along the riverbank during the process of new construction. In the case of this particular set of remains I am, of course, one of the world's three leading experts, though no one else at the scene would ever, could ever, imagine my connection to it.

According to the protocol of these things, there aren't too many people down here. The workers and cops and other curious onlookers are mostly up the slope, above us. This is to avoid any further trampling of possible evidence (which is really moot in this case, since the entire area has been pummeled by workers and their machines and anyway, the river would have washed everything away decades ago, but protocol is what it is). Lewandowski stands beside me. Two of his colleagues, scene investigators, technicians they are, from the Scientific Investigations Unit, are closer to the widening pit, the grave, peering in. They have their tools beside them in important-looking red metal cases, brushes and powders and glassine envelopes and so forth, but they are not doing the pickiest work here. That is left to a woman named Shelley-Jo Janson, Ph.D., a forensic anthropologist and professor at MCOT, the local medical college (where I also teach part time). I called her as soon as I got the call, though I knew immediately what it was. If I hadn't, it might have suggested some slight peculiarity because in these cases of long-buried corpses she is usually involved—she being better at unearthing old human debris and reading the subtle messages from it than even I. Everyone in the business of exhumation and investigation in this city knows it. My urge, of course, was to control the scene. But it has been twenty-five years since this body was buried and I must trust in the obfuscation that that much time renders on all things organic.

I knew in fact several months ago that this moment was coming. A chill crept through me when I read that these condos had been approved and were moving into the development stage, and again when I drove by and saw the equipment being unloaded. I was amazed frankly that the spot had lain unclaimed and unused for this long, and that the river hadn't unearthed any bones in the meantime (though Brigman took care to dig it deep).

Several sets of portable halogen lights encircle us now and serve the dual purpose of not only creating an oasis of high daylight in the deepening dusk of this early September evening (strangely within a calendar week or so of when Brigman and Donny dug the hole), but of warming us some, too—the air not only holds a chill now but the sky is drizzling rain as well. It's a sloppy time and place—not at all unlike the morning when this body was buried—and my feet in the high rubber Wellingtons I wear to such scenes have sunk several inches into the mud. I look up for a moment at the river and the city across it and can see only the silhouette of the skyline now against the fading western sky, and of the great bridge that still stands, of the spot from which Jessi nearly leapt those years ago.

We live in the mansion, strange as that may sound. It hasn't changed much. The pool's been upgraded, the driveway repaved, the decor updated, that sort of thing. The trees are bigger, though that old willow had to be taken down a few years ago. I like to say that we bought it from Ted but we didn't—he gave it to us when we moved back, just signed it over. He went into semiretirement not long after that, at sixty-three, and bought a place in Coconut Grove, Florida, not far from his brother. That was ten years ago. He spends most of his time down there, but comes up for holidays and every summer stays with us for at least a month. He has a reason, you see, beyond us. Her name is Jennifer. She was born in 1989.

We hadn't planned it, hadn't even dared to hope really that we'd ever have time for a family. But it happened as these things do, and it has been wonderful for us.

Jessi has talked to Jennifer about her grandmother. I sat with them once several years ago as they thumbed through one of the photo albums Ted left behind (we inherited much of what they'd acquired), when Jennifer asked who that was, and Jessi told her. Jenny of course asked where Joyce was, and Jessi said that Joyce had died when Jenny was very young. I smiled at the lie. She asked me if I knew Joyce and I said I had, and that I thought they'd have liked each other very much.

One of the techs looks up at me. I step forward. They've turned up a piece of duct tape. No sign of the quilts, just the tape. Amazing how indestructible the stuff is. It does not give me a good feeling. I have to wonder what else has remained undissolved, unabsorbed, still identifiable after all this time. Shelley-Jo looks up from the hole.

"It'll be pretty intact," she says.

I nod and step away again, back a few paces to where Lewandowski smokes a cigar. The homicide guys have this habit at scenes of decomposition. The cigar blocks out much of the stench. But there will be no stench here, the body being buried far too long. Bones, I suspect, and bits of tape are all we will find. Possibly some clothing if he wore synthetics. That frankly is what concerns me most. Did Brigman think to take out the wallet and any other identifying contents of the pockets? Could he have possibly imagined that twenty-five years hence the corpse would come back to the surface to tell some of its tale, with me as its audience? And even if we can identify Ron, will there be anything tying him to us? To Joyce? Was a missing persons report ever filed for the man? I don't know these things. I kneel again, find my spot and my peace, pull my coat around me, and wait.

He's sixty-eight now by the way, Brigman is, and looks every day of it. He lives in the same house in the south end. The neighborhood got even worse after I moved out but then began to improve, and has become again the sort of place I remember from when my mother was alive. We've had work done on the house to keep the outside looking good, and even persuaded him finally to get rid of some of the debris from his collection.

The tech glances up again, at me and then at Shelley-Jo, and when she gives him the okay he reaches with a thin extendable metal rod into the hole and hooks something out. It is a beer can. I had forgotten that, that they were drinking and tossing the empties into the hole. Even Brigman wasn't prescient or cynical enough to predict DNA analysis. I'm not worried about that, though—it would have broken down years ago. I'm more concerned about lingering latent prints. It's a long shot but possible, given that the cans haven't rusted. I'd have guessed they would, but the aluminum content Budweiser used in 1978 was apparently already high. (Did they wear gloves? I can't remember.) What the cans really will do is help date the digging. There'll be BIN numbers or something like that. It's a big find for us, the authorities, and one that will lie utterly beyond my control. Brigman will have to take his chances with the cans. I always said his drinking would catch up with him.

Another can comes out, and then another. The techs bag each

separately and label them and set them side by side on the ground. It feels strange to see these things unearthed, and to remember.

The first hint of bone peeks through now, where the chest plate should be, given the location of the head and assuming the body's still roughly intact. Could Ron have imagined it'd come to this? What I am especially curious about is how it happened—and that will, of course, be strictly up to me to determine. Was it a blow struck in the heat of conflict, a bash to the head maybe? Or something more coldly planned—a slashed throat, a garroting injury. I've always leaned toward the former—I couldn't quite see Brigman gunning for him in some premeditated way but I can certainly imagine once his anger was engaged what he could have done. Woe to Ron at that point.

When Shelley-Jo sits back on her heels it's the sign that we have arrived at some moment of significance. But when she looks at me and says, "You can see her now," I'm confused. Shelley's never been in the habit of referring to uncategorized corpses in the feminine, as if they're ships or something. It's usually not too hard to tell . . .

I feel something then, a shifting, a simultaneous shrinking and expansion as if I am both fading away from the earth and rocketing back through time, all the time of my life, at once. I walk to the lip of the grave and look in. Yellow is what's most immediately striking. The midsection of the corpse has been uncovered, from the bottom of the rib cage to the top of the femurs, and you can make out bits of unabsorbed yellow cloth. Still, I am confused. And then I look at this pelvic girdle that Shelley has so carefully laid bare and I can see in an instant, as she could as well, that it is clearly and without doubt the pelvis of a woman, and probably a woman who bore at least one child.

It is not unlike that moment when I found the video camera in Joyce's upstairs armoire on that long distant afternoon and felt the weight of time cascading down upon me, only this is bigger than that. I stagger, am staggered, actually clutch at my chest because I cannot breathe. I stumble backward and trip and sit down hard in the mud, and I must be gasping like a landed fish because immediately people are at my side bending over me—Lewandowski, the techs. They think I'm having a heart attack, and Lewandowski is on his radio already putting in a call.

TWENTY

The plan must have begun to find its form (in perhaps only a few mumbled words, a hinted-at image, a vague promise) during that night I spent in the hospital after my beating at the head and feet of Ron. Imagine it—in the darkest hours as I lay bruise-brained and gash-scalped and broken-boned, maybe dying for all they knew, Brigman and Ted finally met. Brigman, with much to be pissed off at but also full of desires and frustrations and a deeper longer burning anger at the way the world had messed him up, and Ted with so many things to manage, and desires of his own. Brigman might have been chilly at first but Ted with his sensitivity to how anyone viewed him would have immediately begun to reverse this. And he knew which buttons to push. I can hear him talking about the Rouge plant, his dad. Brigman perhaps then mentioned the Corps and from there Ted had him. At some point in the course of the night the combination of Ted's wealth and his prodigious abilities of persuasion and maybe a never-before-recounted version of the story of how he really lost his hand, and Brigman was overwhelmed. Or so I think, at first.

But sitting there in the mud watching Shelley-Jo dig, Lewandowski still at my side, I think again. Brigman, who has never been anyone's fool, must have realized at some point that he was involved in a negotiation, a strange and subtle and dangerous one, and fur-thermore that what was at stake was nothing less than the future of all of us. He always liked to play the dumb gearhead, but my guess is that he caught the whiff of fear in Ted—of a lawsuit or of being exposed, of god forbid being disgraced in the papers—and with nothing but his instinct to guide him played it as it came, and negotiated my future.

It would have begun, of course, with Ted filling Brigman in on what was happening between me and Joyce. And how it was Joyce, not him, who'd been paying Ron to harass me. It wouldn't've taken Brigman long to absorb all of this and grasp the full ramifications, understand the possible consequences.

On what, then, did they agree? What did Ted promise him? I can't be sure, of course. And it would have been couched at that early stage in the vaguest terms—"It has to be stopped between them," Ted might have said, "whatever that entails."

"Well," Brigman could have answered, "shit can happen."

And then from Ted something like "Syd's a bright boy. I like him in spite of all this. If things . . . turn out the right way, I'd be happy to see him get into med school."

"But the money . . ."

"Yes, well, that doesn't have to be an issue. Assuming things work out."

Whatever. It's all conjecture. But I think that by the time I came to in the morning, the deal had been made—Joyce and I would be given one more chance to stop, and if we didn't, then shit would be made to happen. The fact that I'd just been put in the hospital left the perfect cover—Brigman could rage and marshal Donny and all the time I'd believe that Ron was the object of their wrath.

And what of him, of Ron? Did he simply go away when Joyce's checks stopped coming? Or did Ted track him down and make it worth his while to relocate to some far-off place where he'd never run the risk of my bumping into him by chance or glimpsing him on the street?

Of course the deal would all have been jeopardized when Jessi discovered me at Joyce's apartment. By the time they knew that I wasn't going to stop with Joyce, it was too late, the damage Ted feared had already been wrought. And it very nearly ended there, on the bridge. But (unwittingly) I did my part, pulled it out, got her down, so the deal could play out. I wonder if I'd stopped seeing Jessi, let it fall away, if Ted would have carried through with his part of it. He'd've had grounds not to. But Brigman would have understood, as I did when I began my own confrontations with Ted, who had more to lose, and might've brought some pressure to bear. Who knows? The way things happened, it didn't matter. We all became family.

What I wonder is who killed her. Did Ted use some undetectable poison? Did Brigman strangle her? Or perhaps did Ted hire someone else to do the actual deed, then have Brigman and Donny clean it up? And now the question is—can I figure it out? And do I want to?

The medics arrive and pick their way down the trail and over to our little party. My b.p.'s slightly elevated. Heart sounds fine. I tell them I have low blood sugar and they seem to buy it. They give me a Hershey bar and leave.

When I step over to look again, to begin my own work of inspecting these remains, of deciding exactly what happened to this victim, this woman, this Joyce of my memory and my life, Detective Lewandowski comes with me, his elbow nearly brushing mine—this is I'm sure only in case I have another dizzy spell, but I can't help feeling that his old sniffer is telling him that something's up here.

It is late now. I have only one light on, over the tray that holds the rubberized bag that holds the bones I've been idly arranging into some approximation of their original orientation. I am looking at them and at the bits of yellow cloth, that sun dress she was wearing in her new apartment on the last day I saw her, when my wife steps into the lab. Though I'm sitting with her mother, it is her I've been thinking about, and what I am going to say. What happened back then has lain like some force, hidden, buried, gone for all appearances from the world. But not vanquished. And now it has been resurrected, at least for me because I have a dilemma—what do I tell her? Anything? Everything? I don't know.

"Jessi," I say. She smiles and sits on a stool by the door. Though she spent her time with them when she had to, she's not in love with the dead. She visits here only rarely, and usually when she can't help it for some reason.

She says, "It's very late."

"Yes."

"Dennis called me." They know each other. Lewandowski was a patient of hers for a time after his divorce.

"Ah," I say. "Making a big deal out of nothing."

"What happened?" The light filtering in from the hallway illuminates one side of her face, so that I can just make out her expression.

"We had an exhumation down by the river."

"To you, I mean."

"Low blood sugar."

"Right."

These bones do have an odor, but the human part of it is faint and overwhelmed by the pungent smell of the earth. I pull up the edges of the bag and begin to zip it closed.

"Is that it?"

"Yes. It was there a long time. Several decades."

"Who is it?"

I'm about to say I don't know when I look at her and understand that she will know I'm lying. I don't say anything.

"Is it her?"

It stuns me. And yet it makes sense, a horrible logical sense.

"It hasn't changed much, really," I say, "that part of the river. Until now. It's where they're putting in those new condos."

"Then you've been there before."

"A long time ago."

She is silent for a long moment, and then she says, "Oh, god," and in it I hear a cracking, a crying that wants to come out but knows it must wait.

"I followed them," I say, "Brigman and Donny, and watched them dig. It was bundled up, though, so you couldn't see who. I thought it was him. Ron."

"The one she hired to beat you up?"

"Yes. How do you know that?"

"Is that what Brigman told you, that it was him?"

"Well, that's who he was going after. And he told me it was over—"

"What'd you think, that she just left?"

"Yes."

"Oh, Syd, she would never. You were so blind."

"Apparently."

I am frightened all over again, not for her now, not at the thought of having to broach this never-before-discussed subject and of having to open those wounds again, but for me. Me, I, Syd Redding, who all along it turns out was the one left in the dark.

"That night," she says, and I know precisely which one she means, "I drove for a long time. I was insane. I would have killed her if I'd seen her. I would have killed you. I felt like everything had been taken away from me. Or worse, that I'd never even had it. I'd just been fooled, strung along, and by the two people I maybe cared the most about in the world. In the end, though, I had nowhere else to go. So I came home.

"It was dark, but there was a truck in the driveway. I'd never seen it. A blue truck with toolboxes on the sides.

"Inside, it was quiet but I knew someone was there. Dog wasn't there, which was strange. I went upstairs and heard something in their room, and went back, and that's when I saw them. My dad and yours, and Donny. Standing together.

"Then I saw her."

"Her?"

"She was lying on the bed, very still. They were looking at her.

And I knew what was happening, and what had happened, and what was going to. It was like the universe opened, and for a horrid moment I saw everything exactly for what it was, and understood it. And I knew they hadn't done it yet. That she was still alive."

Ted had sedated her. That's what it was. It would've been easy then—a pillow over the face, a bolus of potassium into a vein, whatever. I won't be able to tell now.

"What'd you do?"

I can see in the light from the hallway that her face is wet, but her voice is steady. "I left."

"Did they see you?"

"I don't think so. No one's ever said anything. I drove and drove again, through the rest of the night, until by morning I was crazy. I knew what I'd done, what I'd let happen. And then I was sorry. I wanted her back. I wanted you back. But you were gone, everyone was gone . . ."

She is a handsome woman, Jessi, in the way of her mother, though they do not really look alike. Jenny, I think, will look more like Joyce when she grows up.

My throat feels thick. "From where they buried her," I say, "there's a clear view of the bridge. We saw all the lights. I knew it was you."

She can no longer speak. I slide the drawer closed and snap off my gloves and stand and walk to her. What else am I going to do? What else is there? She takes me in, holds me in a way that I think she has not done ever in our marriage, or in the years leading up to it, not since the times we made love before the bridge, when Joyce was still alive. Then she used to hold me so tightly sometimes that I could not draw breath, as if she was afraid that letting go meant I would never come back.

An SIU tech will call in a few days to say they came up mostly empty on the cans. I will laugh and ask him if that's a pun. As it happened, they were able to figure that the cans were sold sometime in 1978, but it hasn't led them anywhere.

"There's actually a partial on one of them, a smudged thumb it looks like. We managed to pick up three points, ran it through the AFIS, but nothing came." Which means it wasn't Brigman's, because he's in the system so he'd have come up. The tech says, "We'd have to have something to compare . . ."

But we don't, we won't, because Donny's never been in and at this point I doubt if he ever will be. I think Chloe knows the truth. I mean I'd never have guessed that but looking back at it, looking at her relationship with Jessi, which has remained close all these years, and at how she never again mentioned anything after that time in our kitchen, I think she figured it out, or Jessi told her. So I might tell Chloe to just make sure that Donny never gets fingerprinted for anything or if he's going to, to cut his thumbs off first. She'll understand.

A few days after that I will dig through the boxes of my belongings that have been moldering in our attic for these years, and I will find the note from Joyce that Ted gave me the night of the last day that I ever saw her. I will sit down one day with it when I am home alone and turn to a page in the photo album of some shots of Jessi when she was little, and on which are written a few words in Joyce's hand, the date, the place, and I will compare the note to it, and realize though I am no expert that the handwriting in the note does not match the handwriting on the photos.

Sometime after that then when I have reason to be at St. V's (which I do from time to time) I will slip downstairs to where the laboratory still has its home, and I will saunter back to the Chemistry Department, which is still to this day managed by Barb Lancioni. She has held that position now for twenty years. I'll poke around a little, make small talk with the techs until I see something she's written, a memo, old and yellowish now, taped up by the door. And I will see that the handwriting looks pretty similar to the note I have.

I will think of confronting Ted and Brigman, will even convince myself at times that I will do it. I'll think the whole thing through again and again. Who was lying? Did Joyce hire Ron out of selfishness, to keep me to herself? Or was it Ted all along as I thought, and did he just manipulate things at the end to cover up the murder of a wife whose desires had passed from titillating to tiresome to jeopardizing their daughter? And deeper even than that—who of the two of them really needed to play the game? Was it Ted's compulsion to watch, to see his wife as that kind of object of desire, or was it Joyce's to be seen in that way? In the end, who was the true narcissist?

In any case, what is certain is that they conspired, all of them, Ted and Brigman and Donny and Jessi and Chloe, in a murder and its coverup. It is a horror almost beyond imagining because it involves everyone I love in the world.

But that's wrong. There is someone who remains outside it, unsullied. It is an irony but in the same way that Ted saw Joyce as a danger to his daughter, and so betrayed her, I find that I must betray her, too. Because everything, everything, will be jeopardized if I don't. For that reason, I will not ask. I will see Joyce buried again, unrecognized and unredeemed. In a few more years our Jennifer will graduate from Jessi's alma mater, and we will buy her a large and expensive gift, as her grandfather did for Jessi. It'll be a Volvo, I think. I trust, though, that she will not one day sit in it with a boy and tell him that her father gave it to her in lieu of love, because that is not the case and I know that she knows it. Ours is a different world.

ABOUT THE AUTHOR

CRAIG HOLDEN is the author of four previous novels: *The River Sorrow, The Last Sanctuary, Four Corners of Night,* and *The Jazz Bird.* He lives in Michigan.